HARLEQUIN®
Presents

To all readers of Harlequin Presents

Thank you for your loyal
custom throughout 2006.

We look forward to bringing you the best
in intense, international and provocatively
passionate romance in 2007.

Happy holidays, and all good wishes
for the New Year!

D0724277

Kim Lawrence

SANTIAGO'S
LOVE-CHILD

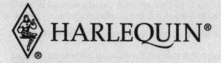

HARLEQUIN®

TORONTO • NEW YORK • LONDON
AMSTERDAM • PARIS • SYDNEY • HAMBURG
STOCKHOLM • ATHENS • TOKYO • MILAN • MADRID
PRAGUE • WARSAW • BUDAPEST • AUCKLAND

ISBN-13: 978-0-373-12593-7
ISBN-10:   0-373-12593-3

SANTIAGO'S LOVE-CHILD

First North American Publication 2006.

Copyright © 2005 by Kim Lawrence.

www.eHarlequin.com

Printed in U.S.A.

All about the author…
Kim Lawrence

Though lacking much authentic Welsh blood, **KIM LAWRENCE** comes from English/Irish stock. She was born and brought up in north Wales. She returned there when she married, and her sons were both born on Anglesey, an island off the coast. Though not isolated, Anglesey is a little off the beaten track, but lively Dublin, which Kim loves, is only a short ferry ride away.

Today they live on the farm her husband was brought up on. Welsh is the first language of many people in this area and Kim's husband and sons are all bilingual—she is having a lot of fun, not to mention a few headaches, trying to learn the language!

With small children, the unsocial hours of nursing didn't look attractive, so encouraged by a husband who thinks she can do anything she sets her mind to, Kim tried her hand at writing. Always a keen Harlequin reader, it seemed natural for her to write a romance novel—now she can't imagine doing anything else.

She is a keen gardener and cook and enjoys running—often on the beach, as living on an island the sea is never very far away. She is usually accompanied by her Jack Russell, Sprout—don't ask, it's long story!

CHAPTER ONE

AFTER trying to sell an idea for ten minutes straight most people would have given up. Dan Taylor wasn't one of them. Some people said that what he lacked in flair he made up for in determination. They were essentially correct.

Santiago Morais, who was considered to have more than his fair share of flair, listened to the younger man explain again why it wasn't just *necessary* for Santiago to make up the numbers this weekend, it was his *duty*.

'No.'

The 'No' wasn't the sort of no that could be confused with maybe, and it wasn't encouraging that the enigmatic expression on Santiago's lean features had given way to mild irritation.

Actually Dan was a little taken aback by Santiago's lack of co-operation. He was showing the sort of stony indifference that Dan had expected five years earlier when he had turned up at the London offices of Morais International. The only thing he'd had going for him then had been a tenuous—*very* tenuous—family link with the Morais family.

He had expected to be thrown out on his ear. Getting to see the man himself had been just as hard as he had expected. When they had come face to face, his resolve had almost deserted him. Santiago was younger than he had expected and much, much tougher.

Faced with a dark, cynical and very chilly stare Dan had instinctively dumped his carefully prepared speech and said instead, 'Look, there's absolutely no reason you should

7

give me a job just because some great-aunt of mine married some distant uncle of your mother's. I'm not qualified—in fact I've never finished anything I started in my life—but if you gave me a chance you wouldn't regret it. I'd give it all I had and then some. I have something to prove.'

'You have something to prove?' The voice, deep and barely accented, made Dan jump.

'I'm not a loser.'

The figure behind the desk got to his feet and became correspondingly more intimidating; this man was seriously tall and was built like an Olympic rower. For a long uncomfortable moment Santiago just looked at Dan in silence, those spookily penetrating eyes not giving a clue to what he was thinking.

'Right, sorry to have bothered you…'

'Eight-thirty Monday.'

Dan's jaw dropped as he swung back. *What did you say?*

One of Santiago's dark brows lifted. 'If you want a job, be here Monday morning at eight-thirty.'

Dan sank into the nearest chair. 'You won't regret this,' he vowed.

Dan had come good on his promise. He had quickly proved his worth and, perhaps more surprisingly, a friendship had developed between the two men. A friendship that had survived Dan leaving the company and setting up on his own two years earlier.

Dan adopted an injured expression as he looked across at his Spanish distant cousin, who had put down a file he'd been reading to say something in his native tongue into a Dictaphone. Actually it could have been one of several languages; Santiago was fluent in five.

'I must say I think you're being pretty callous about this.'

'If by callous you mean I will not spend a weekend

amusing a fat, boring and mentally unstable woman—I'm quoting you here—so that you can have your Rebecca to yourself…I am indeed callous.'

'*Rachel*, and the friend isn't mentally unstable exactly. I think she's just having a breakdown or something.'

'You're really tempting me now, but the answer is still no, Daniel.'

'If you'd met Rachel you wouldn't be so heartless.'

'And is your Rachel beautiful?'

'Very, and don't look at me like that. This isn't some casual affair. She's *the one*; I just know she is.' His expression grew indignant when Santiago responded to his emotional admission with a cynical smile that was only slightly less corrosive than neat nitric acid. 'I'd have thought you'd have been more sympathetic considering…' Dan continued falteringly.

Santiago abandoned his attempt to carry on working and pushed his thick sable hair back from his brow. 'Considering what?'

'Aren't you getting married?'

'At some point I imagine it will be necessary.' The exquisite irony of him continuing the precious Morais family name was not lost on him.

'You know what I mean. Aren't you marrying that hot little singer who I keep seeing you photographed with.'

'That hot little singer has an agent with a vivid imagination. Susie is not in love with me.'

Dan's expression grew curious. 'So it's just…'

'None of your business.'

'Fair enough, but I still think you're being totally unreasonable. I'm asking you to spend a weekend in a cute cottage, not donate bone marrow! Look…look,' he said, reaching into his pocket and extracting a photo. 'Isn't she gorgeous? And, as for her being older, I *like* older women…' he added defensively as he shoved the photo under Santiago's nose.

With a sigh Santiago took the creased item from the younger man's fingers and dutifully glanced at the slightly out-of-focus image of a tall blonde who looked to him like many other tall blondes.

'Yes, she is very…' He stopped, the colour seeping steadily from his olive-toned skin as he looked at the person half concealed by Dan's girlfriend.

'Are you feeling all right?' Dan asked, thinking of Santiago's father, who had dropped dead at fifty-five from a massive heart attack several years earlier.

Santiago hadn't inherited his dad's looks, generous girth or taste for copious amounts of brandy—the old man had by all accounts been a bit of a sleaze—but who knew what else he had inherited?

Like maybe a propensity to heart disease and dropping down dead!

Dan had started to try and remember if you bashed someone who stopped breathing on the chest, or gave them mouth to mouth, when Santiago's eyes lifted. He looked bleak, but much to Dan's relief not about to expire any time soon.

'I'm fine, Daniel.' Santiago wasn't about to reveal that he'd recognized the woman in the photograph. 'This woman here, she is the friend who will be there this weekend?' he enquired casually as he indicated the figure in the background.

'Yeah, that's Lily,' Dan admitted without enthusiasm. 'Rachel's had her staying at her place for the past three weeks. They go way back. I never see Rachel alone. Wherever she goes, there's Lily. I don't think she likes men…she *definitely* doesn't like me. Must be the husband dumping her has made her all weird.'

'Her husband left her…?'

Dan nodded. 'Not too sure of the details, but presumably that's what made her fall apart.'

Santiago's eyes lifted. 'Are they divorced?'

'Like I said, I don't know the details. I had a colleague lined up for this weekend to keep her out of our hair, but he got mumps, of all things!'

'That was inconsiderate of him,' Santiago murmured sarcastically, thinking fast and hard—something he was well equipped to do.

'I'm not saying he did it on purpose, but, hell-fire, Santiago, I've been planning this weekend for weeks, ever since I bought the ring.'

'You are going to propose?' He watched as Dan looked self-conscious and thought, *I hope she's not a total bitch.* Being Lily's friend was not the best of recommendations.

'Six years is a very small age gap.'

'Insignificant,' Santiago agreed obediently, amused that it was something as minor as an age difference that bothered his young friend. 'This alters things,' he mused out loud.

'It does?' Dan sounded cautious.

'Being a romantic—'

'*Since when?*'

'I will come and keep this…*Lily*…company.'

Dan was so grateful that it took Santiago ten minutes to get rid of him.

When Dan finally left, Santiago took the photograph he had slipped surreptitiously into his pocket and laid it on the desk. Hands pressed on the polished rosewood surface, he leaned forward, his eyes trained on the barely distinguishable features of the woman in the background. A quiver of movement tightened the contours of his impossibly symmetrical features. When admirers attributed that symmetry to generations of aristocratic inbreeding, Santiago could barely repress his amusement.

Lily's hair looked dark in the snapshot, but Santiago knew it was a medium brown, not a boring matt brown, but a fascinating intermingling of shades ranging from golden blonde to warm, rich russet.

That heart-shaped little face—thinner than he recalled—those big, kittenish blue eyes, and soft, seductive mouth didn't look as though they belonged to a woman who had the morals of an alley cat.

She had made a fool of him.

But, as Santiago had told himself many times over the last months, he had the consolation of knowing that he had had a lucky escape. *Lucky me!*

He wasn't married to this heartless little cheat—*someone else was.* Another man enjoyed the expertise of those soft lips. Someone else slept with his head cushioned on those soft, warm breasts at night. That man was entitled to touch pearly skin that smelt of roses and vanilla, and wake up with pale, smooth limbs wrapped around him.

Another man was listening to her lies and believing them.

Someone else, but not me.

Oddly enough, thoughts of his lucky escape did not make Santiago feel like breaking into spontaneous song.

Then he remembered Daniel's words and realised that it was possible nobody was enjoying the carnal delights of her voluptuous body. Recalling what a sensual little thing she had been, he doubted this situation would last for long.

He looked at his hands clenched into white-knuckled fists and rotated his head to ease the tension that had crept into his shoulders and neck. He was over the woman; it was the memory of his own criminal gullibility that plagued him, that stopped him fully enjoying what life had to offer. The obvious way to restore equilibrium was to face his problem. He needed what the psychologists called closure, and what he, in the privacy of his own thoughts, called seeing Lily get what she deserved.

Now, thanks to Dan, he had the chance.

Staring out of the window, seeing none of the panoramic view over the city, he mulled over what he had learnt and wondered how it could be used to his advantage. Apparently Lily was going through a rough patch. The protective instincts that sprang into life at the thought of her vulnerability didn't survive more than a split second before good sense reasserted itself.

He smiled grimly. Maybe it was Lily's turn to reap some of what she had sown…? Or maybe her present *breakdown* was part of some elaborate scam, which, knowing her as he did, was entirely possible.

Though he had nothing to prove, it would be good to confirm what he already knew: *that he was over Lily.*

'You've been crying.'

Lily, who had thought she was alone, jumped at the accusation and gave a surreptitious sniff before lifting her head. 'No,' she mumbled, pinning a determined smile on her blotchy face, 'it's this darned hay fever.'

Her friend sighed. 'You don't get hay fever, Lily,' she retorted, dropping her designer handbag on the floor and easing one shoe off with a sigh.

Lily watched the second four-inch heel follow suit as Rachel shrank to a willowy five ten. Her cheeks began to ache as she continued to smile brightly to compensate for her blotchy appearance.

She blew her nose defiantly. 'Well, I do now,' she insisted.

Rachel lifted her artfully darkened brows and released a theatrical sigh, but didn't press the point.

'If you say so,' she said, wincing as she rubbed first one aching foot and then the other against her slim calves. 'Now, what shall we do tonight?'

'I fancy an early night, actually.'

'Early night! You've had early nights for the past week.' She looked her friend up and down through narrowed eyes, mentally chucking the top Lily was wearing in the bin— no self-respecting charity shop would want it—and getting her into something, preferably low cut, in a pastel shade maybe...? A nice soft smoky blue would bring out the incredible shade of her eyes.

'It's definitely time you let your hair down, Lily. It'll do us both good,' she contended.

Lily guiltily noted for the first time the lines of fatigue around the older woman's eyes. 'Bad day?'

'Sometimes I wonder why I ever became an accountant,' she admitted.

'The six-figure salary...?'

Rachel grinned. 'I get that because I'm brilliant at what I do. And I won't bother trying to explain to someone who can't even add up *with* a calculator that numbers are sexy. Now, about tonight. Dan has this really sweet mate...single, solvent...admittedly he's no Brad Pitt, but then—'

'Beggars can't be choosers...?'

Rachel adopted an expression of mock gravity. 'Well, I was going to say, *Who is?* But now you mention it women who don't exfoliate regularly, Lily, have to be realistic.' She turned her frowning scrutiny on the younger woman's fair-skinned face. 'Actually, considering your skin-care regime consists of splashing a bit of soap and water on your face, you have the most disgustingly gorgeous skin,' she observed enviously. 'A bit of decent foundation would totally disguise those freckles,' she prophesied, frowning at the bridge of Lily's small, tip-tilted nose. 'Still, some men like freckles. Shall I ring Dan and—'

Lily knew one man who had said he liked her freckles, though she suspected they, like everything else about her, would disgust him now.

'*No!*' Rachel's eyebrows lifted and Lily added more moderately, 'I appreciate what you're trying to do, I really do, but, to be honest, a man is the last thing I need right now.'

It was easy to figure out what she *didn't* need—blind dates featured pretty high on this list. What she *did* need was a much more difficult proposition!

'*Need* and *want* are not always the same thing.'

'This time they are,' Lily insisted quietly.

Rachel looked exasperated and glanced absently at a message on her mobile phone before sliding it back into her bag. 'What are you going to do? Take a vow of celibacy?'

Lily ignored Rachel's question. 'Actually, I was thinking it might be time for me to go home.' Home…but for how much longer?

Lily deliberately pushed the subject of her uncertain future to the back of her mind.

It wasn't easy. Her marital home was on the market, and according to the agents a couple were making interested noises, which, considering their viewing, was nothing short of a miracle.

Lily's thoughts drifted back to the occasion three weeks earlier. Rachel had unexpectedly arrived when she had been halfway through showing the prospective purchasers around. Her friend had taken one look at her, and had calmly informed the startled pair that they would have to come back another day. She had then proceeded to escort them firmly off the property.

Rachel had then packed Lily a bag, arranged a sitter for the cat and asked a neighbour to water the plants. Lily had just sat there and watched her. She supposed her listless inertia had been a symptom of whatever Rachel had seen in her face.

The break had served its purpose, but now, despite the tears this afternoon, Lily was feeling less fragile. She no longer felt so...*disconnected*. She wasn't sure whether to be relieved or not. Being grounded was painful, you had to think about things you'd prefer not to and make decisions... For months now, she realised, she'd just been drifting. She hadn't even begun to look for somewhere to live. All she'd done was sign everything that Gordon's solicitor had sent her.

Yes, it was definitely about time she stood on her own feet.

Rachel didn't agree.

'You can't go home yet. I've got things planned.'

Lily, who didn't like the sound of 'things' frowned suspiciously. She really wished that her friend hadn't taken on the role of social secretary with such zeal. *'Things...?'*

Rachel acted as if she hadn't heard. 'God, but these shoes are murder,' she complained, picking up the culprits, stilettos with black and pink bows.

'Then don't wear them.' It seemed the obvious solution to Lily, who liked clothes but wasn't as much of a slave to fashion as her friend.

'Are you kidding? They make my legs look hot.'

Lily looked at the legs in question and observed honestly, 'Your legs would look hot in wellingtons, Rachel.' She glanced down at her own legs, currently concealed under denim. They were pretty good as legs went, but they weren't in the same class as Rachel's, which stopped traffic on a regular basis.

'Yes, they would, wouldn't they?'

Lily smiled. There was something oddly endearing about her friend's complacent vanity.

'But enough about my legs.' With a little pat of one taut, tanned thigh through her short summer skirt, she turned her attention to Lily, who in turn looked wary, an expression her friend had observed always appeared when the conversation got even faintly personal.

Such tight-lipped reserve was something Rachel found hard to understand. If she had been through hell and back like Lily, she would have *wanted* to get it off her chest, but all her attempts to encourage Lily to let it out had failed miserably.

'Don't you think you'd feel a lot better if you talked about it?'

They both knew what 'it' was: Lily's divorce—the ink was still wet on that—and her miscarriage earlier that year.

CHAPTER TWO

FOR a split second Lily was tempted to tell Rachel; the urge quickly passed.

Rachel didn't know half the story and the truth was so shocking that she couldn't predict how even her broad-minded friend would react to the unvarnished version.

Besides, the habits of a lifetime were hard to break and 'sharing feelings' had been encouraged during Lily's childhood about as much as spontaneous hugging!

If she had let her feelings show, her grandmother's impatient response had been, 'Nobody likes a whiner, Lily.' Lily had learnt not to whine. Her crying had always been done behind closed doors.

'Nothing to talk about.'

'Nobody does the stiff upper lip these days, you know, Lily. All that being reserved does is give you an ulcer.'

'My stomach feels fine.' Lily placed her hand against the curve of her belly and discovered with a sense of surprise that she had lost a lot of the soft, feminine roundness she had always hated.

The softness that Santiago had professed to find sexy and feminine.

She knew from experience that there were times when fighting the flashbacks did no good, that it was easier on those occasions just to go with the flow. Lily, dimly conscious of Rachel's voice in the background, felt her eyelids grow heavy as she allowed the bitter-sweet memories to wash over her.

She had perfect, total, painful recall of the heat in his

incredible eyes as he had tipped her face up to his and smiled a slow, sexy smile as he had drawn her against him, fitting his hard angles into her softer curves and murmuring throatily in her ear.

A woman should be soft and round, not hard and angular.

It was humiliating, but a full twelve months after that first scorching kiss and she still couldn't think about it without getting palpitations.

'Well?'

Rachel's impatient voice acted like a lifeline back to the present. Lily grabbed it and held on. While she was fixated on the past the chances of her rebuilding her life were nil.

She dabbed her tongue to the beads of sweat along her upper lip and gave a strained smile as she rubbed her damp palms against her jeans.

'Sorry, I…' *Am pathetic and living in the past? Can't get it into my thick skull he never loved me? All of the above?*

'You weren't listening. I could tell…' Rachel considered her friend's flushed face. 'You look a bit…?'

'I'm fine.' Smile fixed, Lily pushed the intrusive images away without acknowledging them or *his* presence in her head.

'What you need is a nice glass of wine,' Rachel decided. 'Just don't move,' she said, padding over to the big stainless-steel fridge in her bare feet. A moment later she returned with a bottle of Chardonnay and two glasses, which she filled.

'A nice night in…yeah, I can live with that,' she conceded, handing Lily her glass. She curled up comfortably on the sofa and reached for the newspaper. 'I wonder what's on the telly tonight?' Turning over the pages, she suddenly stopped and lowered the broadsheet to the table.

'Now there,' she observed with a lascivious smile, 'is something I wouldn't mind finding in my Christmas stocking.'

'I thought you were in love with your delicious Dan.' Lily laughed, looking over her shoulder to see what hunk her friend was drooling over.

'I'm in love, not blind. Now, *there's* a man who doesn't use a shoebox to file his returns. Look at that mouth and those eyes…' she enthused.

'You can tell about his filing system from his mouth?' Lily teased.

'No, that I can tell by the attention the financial pages give him on a regular basis. I wonder if he's that sexy in real life?' She slung a comical look of entreaty over her shoulder. 'And please don't spoil it by saying it's just good lighting. You're such a disgusting cynic.'

Lily went cold as she looked at the half-page photo showing an unsmiling, dark-eyed man. It was a standard moody black and white shot of an incredibly attractive man. Lily knew that the lighting couldn't begin to do justice to just *how* sexy the man was in real life. It didn't reveal the aura of raw sexuality he projected like a force field.

Aware that some sort of response was expected of her, and hyperventilating wasn't it, Lily cleared her throat. 'He does have something,' she admitted, reading the headline above that pronounced MORAIS LEAVES THE OPPOSITION COUNTING THE COST AGAIN.

Me too, she thought.

'*Something!*' Rachel squealed. 'He is off-the-scale gorgeous. That man,' she said, poking the page with her finger, 'not only looks like he could be quite *deliciously bad* in bed—'

Never again will I mock Rachel's instinct, Lily decided. Of course, Rachel's instinct only told part of the story—as well as being deliciously bad he could also be breathtakingly tender and passionately unrestrained. Lily pressed her hands to her stomach as the muscles deep inside tightened.

'He's also a genuine financial genius. His name is Santiago Morais.' Rachel's smooth brow furrowed. 'He's Italian or—'

'Spanish,' Lily inserted in a flat little voice. 'He's Spanish.' *And I am so over him,* she thought, pressing her hand against her sternum to ease the tight feeling in her chest.

'Yeah, you're right. Since when did you start reading the financial pages, Lily?'

'He makes the gossip columns too,' she said, struggling to keep the bitterness from her voice as an image of the pop star Susie Sebastian, her pouting lips aimed like heat-seeking missiles at a willing male mouth, flashed into her mind.

'That figures. You know, I think I'll spend my next holiday in Spain. You never know, I might bump into Mr Gorgeous. He would carry me off to bed and make mad, passionate love to me.'

Lily half closed her eyes, and saw sun-dappled shadows dancing over a lean golden torso as the breeze stirred the leaves of a tree outside the window. 'For five days straight?'

Rachel angled an amused look at Lily's face. 'Hey, get your own fantasy!' she protested.

Lily blushed, which made Rachel chuckle. 'You have hidden murky depths, girl.'

You have no idea, Lily thought.

For a while after she'd come out of hospital Lily had thought she would never feel anything ever again. Now she wasn't so sure that would have been such a bad thing! Oh, when were things *ever* going to get back to normal? So she could get on with being a librarian who lived in a Devon seaside town.

She knew that it wasn't healthy or constructive to go down the 'what if?' road, but she couldn't help wondering what her life would be like now if she hadn't gone down to the pool that morning all those months ago. It had been such a small decision, but the consequences had been life-changing.

An early-morning swim hadn't seemed sinister or significant, just a good way to clear her head after a long, sleepless night alone in the decadent honeymoon suite of a Spanish five-star hotel, which, rumour had it, had been fully booked up for the next decade or so.

It would have been understandable if the thoughts that had kept her awake had concerned her absent husband. Her husband who hadn't been answering her calls. The *same* husband who had texted her the previous morning to say the problem at work that had forced him to leave her at the airport at the start of their holiday had turned into a crisis and, no, he wouldn't be joining her after all.

Gordon wasn't to know that, following his text, determined to make the best of her holiday to this enchanting area, Lily had booked herself onto an excursion to the charming nearby Renaissance town of Baeza. Places like this were part of the reason she had fallen in love with Andalucia.

She hadn't immediately placed the middle-aged man and his wife bearing down on her as the tour guide was in full flow. Then as she'd looked beyond the shorts and garish shirt she'd recognised a colleague of Gordon's and his wife. She'd vaguely recalled meeting them on a few social occasions.

'Matt…Susan.' She called out to the couple.

They did the usual 'small world, fancy meeting you here'

stuff, and then the older man looked around expectantly. 'Gordon not with you?'

'No, he couldn't get away, I'm afraid.'

If he had, there was no way she'd have got to take this excursion; Gordon wouldn't have budged from the five-star luxury of the hotel. If she had suggested that they go and see the real inland Andalucia, with its olive groves and rolling hills, he would have thought she was crazy.

'Not surprised,' the other man confessed. 'He must be up to his eyes in it with his new venture. I couldn't believe it when I heard on the grapevine he was leaving. I admit, I thought Gordon was a permanent fixture like me.'

Miraculously Lily's smile stayed superglued in place. 'So did I, Matt.'

'And he was a sure bet for that promotion.'

Lily nodded in agreement. 'He did mention that.' One of the few things he had mentioned, it seemed.

'But good for him, I say. You need to be a risk-taker sometimes.' He looked across the square. 'Is that your group moving on?'

'Yes, it is. Lovely to see you.'

Blissfully oblivious to the fact that with a few words he had revealed her marriage to be a total joke, Matt shouted cheerily after her, 'Remember me to Gordon and wish him all the luck in the future.'

He's going to need all the luck he can get when I get hold of him. 'I will,' Lily promised with her best sincere smile.

Of course, she had known for some time that their marriage had problems, but she hadn't suspected until now that they might be insurmountable.

My husband is leading a double life! What the hell is he up to?

At the first opportunity Lily slipped away from her tour

group and sought refuge in the town's delightful flower-filled plaza. She sat in a pavement café and ordered coffee, then, changing her mind, asked instead for wine in her clumsy, faltering Spanish. The proprietor brought a bottle.

She sat sipping the rich-bodied red and thinking about what she was going to do next. Didn't a woman in her situation need a plan of action?

She could run up a credit-card bill, one guaranteed to bring tears to Gordon's eyes. It wouldn't be hard. Gordon had a deep, almost spiritual connection with his wallet—in fact, not to put too fine a point on it, he was as mean as hell!

Then again, she mused, she could take the direct approach and get the next plane home, tell him straight if he didn't want her to walk he'd better come clean about what he'd been up to. But was it a good idea to confront him when she wasn't even sure any more if she *wanted* to save their marriage?

She could always cut the sleeves off his favourite designer suits, give the bottles of wine he'd put down as an investment to the church raffle... But, no, that had been done before by other, more imaginative wronged wives. But wasn't she jumping the gun? Maybe her deepest suspicions were off and another woman wasn't involved.

Sure, because Gordon's never cheated before.

Lily toyed with the idea of sleeping with the first attractive man she saw. It would certainly be one way to have her revenge.

She knew the alcohol was partially responsible for her audacious line of thought, but for a while it was good to feel daring and in charge, not a damned victim.

When the bottle was empty she still hadn't decided what course, if any, to take. The helpful proprietor of the café offered to call her a taxi and for once she thought, *Hang the cost,* and let him.

Given the day's revelations and the fact she spent the rest of the afternoon sleeping off the unaccustomed alcohol, Lily never *expected* to sleep that night, and she didn't, but not for the reason she had anticipated. No, all thoughts of her secretive husband and his mysterious new venture were crowded out of her head by the dark, chiselled features of a total stranger! This probably said something about her character. Lily wasn't sure what, but she doubted it was flattering.

The next morning the solitude of the pool and exercise had the desired therapeutic effect, or so she naively believed at the time. After several slow, steady lengths she succeeded in rationalising what had happened in the hotel restaurant the night before. So she had been the victim of instant lust—it happened, she told herself with a mental shrug. Admittedly never before to her.

It was silly to get hung up about it.

It wasn't as if she had done anything awful like cheat— at least only in her mind. And she suspected every woman who ever laid eyes on the tall, dynamic Spaniard with his sinfully sexy smile and incredible voice was guilty of that.

By the time exhaustion forced her to flip over onto her back and get her breath back Lily had reached the comfortable mental position of concluding she had handled the evening pretty well, under the circumstances.

The *circumstances* being she had hardly been capable of stringing two words together in the man's presence, but there was no need to dwell on that! As for that frisson when their eyes had met and the tug, the feeling of *connection*, she had felt, such things did not happen between total strangers except in her feverish imagination.

Sensual fantasies aside, their brief encounter had actually been pretty much a non-event.

Lying on her back in the water, she couldn't help her thoughts drifting back to the moment she had seen him. Lily involuntarily inhaled as the tall figure with a dark, classically featured face crystallised in her head.

He had achingly perfect, chiselled cheekbones, a proud nose, a strong jaw, dark, smouldering eyes and a sternly sexy mouth that just had to have fuelled countless female fantasies.

She had been lending half an ear to the elderly couple who had invited her to share their table at dinner when she had seen him framed in the doorway.

A tall, dark figure, dressed in a pale linen suit and open-necked shirt that revealed a tantalising section of olive-toned skin and undoubtedly had a designer name hand-stitched into the lining.

It hadn't just been her, lots of people had looked, but Lily had carried on looking a lot longer than most others. She hadn't been able to help herself. The stranger had been quite simply *spectacular*!

He'd been deliciously dark in a typically Spanish way, but nothing else about him had been *typical*! For a start he'd been much taller than the average Spanish male; she'd estimated that he had to be six four or five. Even the way he'd moved, with a fluid animal grace that had made her tummy muscles quiver, had been rivetingly different. His features had been classical, but strong. Her fascinated glance had lingered on his sensually moulded mouth.

It had felt like a long time, but it had probably only been a few seconds, before she'd managed to drag her hungry eyes clear, but in the process she'd connected briefly with his eyes. For a split second the rest of the room had faded away, and something that had felt like a mild electric shock had travelled through her body.

Lily had been utterly overwhelmed by emotions that she hadn't recognised or understood. Rachel would no doubt have identified what she'd been suffering from as lust, but Lily knew it hadn't been that simple.

White and shaking with reaction, she'd examined the pattern in the marble floor. Her heart had continued to race while some inner instinct had told her of his approach. By the time he'd reached her side every nerve ending in her body had been taut with anticipation.

She couldn't even think about it now with a clear head, in the cold light of day without her pulses racing. She hadn't been able to breathe; excitement had lodged itself like a tight fist behind her breastbone. Of course, when he'd walked straight past her as though she were invisible and clasped the elderly man beside her on the shoulder she'd felt every kind of fool.

CHAPTER THREE

AFTER exchanging a few polite words with the couple, who were apparently frequent visitors to the hotel, the handsome stranger had walked away. It had only been later in the evening that Lily had found out his identity—his name was Santiago Morais, and he owned the hotel, and, so it appeared, a whole lot else.

He had barely even acknowledged she was there.

Except for a kind of stiff inclination of his head in her general direction, no eye contact—even the most generous of judges would have to conclude that it had been pretty thin material for a night's steamy fantasies. The eyes across a crowded room, soul-mate stuff had been a product of her overactive imagination.

She was shaking her head over her own pathetic self-delusion as she heaved herself out of the pool and sat, knees up to her chin, eyes closed and head tilted back to catch the warmth of the early-morning rays.

When she opened them the cause of her sleepless night, Santiago Morais, was standing there looking down at her.

'Good morning. I trust you slept well?' In contrast to his formal enquiry there was nothing vaguely formal about the restless febrile glitter she saw in his deep-set, heavy-lidded eyes before he slid a pair of designer shades on.

Lily didn't say anything, partly because the sight of him casually peeling off his shirt had paralysed her vocal cords.

She watched, too shocked to guard her expression as he dragged a hand through his dark hair and set off a sequence of distracting muscle-rippling. He really didn't have an ounce of surplus flesh on his athletically lean frame.

'I didn't sleep well at all,' he revealed without waiting for Lily to answer his question.

'Sorry,' she croaked, thinking he didn't look as if he'd had a disturbed night. He was oozing an indecent degree of vitality, or was that testosterone? Things deep in her pelvis tightened and ached as she focused hazily on his criminally sexy mouth. *Bad idea!*

Don't drool, be objective, Lily, she warned herself severely.

'Did you have a good swim?' he asked, unzipping his jeans to reveal a flat stomach with perfect muscle definition and a light dusting of dark hair.

'I was just leaving.'

He had been watching her…? The thought caused a secret shiver to pass through Lily's body. She lifted her arm in a concealing arc over her tingling nipples, and pulled herself up onto her knees just as the worn denim of his jeans slid down his narrow hips.

As she took in his muscular thighs complete with a light dusting of body hair her breath quickened to the point where she was not so much breathing as noisily gasping for air.

If only for the sake of her own traumatised heart, she knew she ought to avert her eyes. Heaven knew, she tried, but she couldn't; her eyes were glued to his body. He was so beautiful. She could remember feeling awkward, clumsy and overweight in comparison to his sleek hardness.

'I meant to lose some weight for this summer,' she explained, feeling the sudden need to apologise for her appearance.

Above his designer shades Santiago's sable brows lifted. Behind the dark lenses it was hard to see what he was thinking, but she could guess—*Crazy woman, where is security when I need it?*

She smiled to show she was actually sane. 'But you know how it is.' *Stupid, of course he doesn't.*

Her attention was irresistibly drawn back to his body. By this point he had stripped down to a pair of black swimming shorts that left enough to the imagination to send her temperature soaring several degrees.

The sensation she experienced when she looked at his streamlined golden body was a lot as she imagined drowning might be. The inability to breathe; the heavy pounding of her heart...only drowning would feel cold and she was hot...*very* hot! She took a deep, shaky breath as she struggled to get her breathing back on track and averted her eyes from the arrow of dark hair that dived below the waistband of his shorts.

'Why would you want to lose any pounds?'

Lily didn't take Santiago's bewilderment seriously. 'You've got very nice manners, but I know I'm fat,' she explained matter-of-factly. 'I can't even blame it on my genes; apparently my mother was slim.' Her grandmother, who like many people equated extra pounds with laziness, had been fond of regretfully observing that Lily had missed out on her mother's good looks.

'*Fat...!*' His incredulity gave way to laughter, deep, warm laughter. Through the smoky lenses of his sunglasses she was aware of his eyes moving in a broad, caressing sweep down the length of her body. When he reached her toes he released a long, appreciative sigh. 'You are not *fat*!' He dismissed the claim with a contemptuous motion of his hand.

Lily was so startled when, without warning, he dropped down onto his heels until his eyes were almost level with hers that it didn't even occur to her to protest when he reached across and took her chin in his hand.

He looked into her round, startled eyes. His slow smile made her stomach flip. In this enlightened age Lily wasn't sure if *predatory* should be turning her on.

'What you are is soft…' His voice was deep and dark and textured like deepest velvet. She trembled violently as his thumb moved in a circular motion over the apple of her smooth cheek and she experienced another debilitating rush of heat. 'And lush.' His glance settled on her slightly parted lips. 'And very, very feminine. An hourglass figure is something that men will always admire.'

Gordon hadn't thought so, and Lily felt qualified to disagree. 'Not all men,' she contended huskily.

He dismissed this unappreciative minority with a contemptuous shrug. 'Why do you constantly run yourself down?' he wondered, letting his hand fall from her face and frowning.

'I don't,' she protested, placing the back of her hand against the place his fingers had touched her skin and feeling ridiculously bereft.

He looked amused. 'It is obviously an ingrained pattern of behaviour.'

'That's me, a hopeless case. Look, it's been very nice talking to you…' Surreal was much nearer the mark. There was no mystery about why she was hopelessly attracted to him, the mystery was why he should even pretend to feel similarly about her. 'But I really must be—' His deep voice cut smoothly across her.

'Not hopeless, *querida*. An appreciative lover, someone who could teach you to enjoy your own body, could cure you.'

Having begun to get to her feet, Lily sank back down as her legs literally folded beneath her. 'Are you offering?' In her head it sounded ironic, the sort of slick comeback that invited laughter. Unfortunately it actually emerged sounding humiliatingly hopeful.

'And if I was would you be interested?'

Lily didn't smile; she was too busy panicking. To take him seriously would obviously be a major mistake and a direct route to total humiliation. 'I suppose that's your idea of a joke,' she snapped.

'I am not laughing,' he pointed out tautly.

Lily, who had noticed this, swallowed. There was a driven intensity in his manner that she didn't understand, but it excited her anyway. As she stared he lifted a hand and again dragged it through his hair. His brown fingers were long and elegant...sensitive, but strong. He had the sort of hands you would like to look at against the bare flesh of your stomach...other places too.

'You did not know your mother?'

She looked at him startled by his sudden change of direction and she stopped thinking about his fingers on her bare skin.

'You said "apparently" your mother was slim,' he reminded her.

'Did I?' Lily frowned. Her ability to carry on any sort of conversation was severely hampered by the fact that every time she looked at him she experienced a fresh jolt of mind-mushing sexual longing.

'You did.'

'Will you stop doing that?' She snapped, adjusting her towel.

'What?'

'Checking out my cleavage.' Last night he had blanked her, this morning he was mentally undressing her and not trying to hide it. What was going on?

A laugh was drawn from his throat. 'Don't worry. I can

discuss your family and admire your body at the same time.'

'That's an original slant on multi-tasking,' she replied faintly. Inside her chest her heart was fluttering like a trapped animal. 'But I have no desire to discuss my family with you...'

A white wolfish grin split his dark, lean face. 'Then I will settle for admiring your body.'

Lily gave a frustrated little groan and felt a trickle of sweat pool in the valley between her breasts. *What I need is a cold shower,* she thought, picturing cold arrows of water hitting her overheated flesh.

Think cold water... Unfortunately the mental cooling-down process was hampered by the addition of a slickly wet male body in the imaginary shower with her.

'I don't want you to do that either,' she replied hotly.

'Don't you...?'

Working on the basis that it was better to avoid outright lies whenever possible, Lily didn't respond to this husky question. 'Do you always hassle hotel guests this way?' she demanded huskily.

Slowly he shook his head and the twisted smile he gave her was hard to read. 'No, this is actually a unique experience for me.'

The hell of it was she wanted to believe him. She had always despised women who believed slick chat-up lines and here she was wanting to believe that a man who could have any woman he wanted thought she was unique and irresistible. Delusions didn't get any grander than that!

'Just for the record, my mother gave birth to me, and then dumped me with my grandmother, who brought me up. I haven't seen her...*ever*...and as for my father I don't know who he was, but the odds are she didn't either.' *Now why did I tell him that?*

Lily began to get angrily to her feet. This had to be some sort of game. 'I'm not playing,' she muttered from between clenched teeth.

To her way of thinking there was no way a man who possessed a perfect, hard, streamlined, muscular body like Santiago could possibly find anything to admire in her own over-generous curves.

She gave a startled yelp when halfway to her feet the towel she was clutching was unceremoniously wrenched from her fingers.

'Give that back!' she pleaded huskily.

He shook his head, slung the towel carelessly in the pool and removed his shades. His extravagant lashes lifted from the razor-edged curve of his cheekbones to reveal stunning eyes, so dark as to be almost black and flecked by pinpricks of silver. Lily gasped and shivered uncontrollably; the message glimmering in those mesmerising depths was inescapably sensual.

'You didn't ask me why I didn't sleep last night...?'

Raw and driven, his voice drew a low moan from her throat. Lily pressed a hand to the base of her throat where a pulse was hammering away. 'I find hot milk works a treat.'

This sterling advice caused his mouth to spasm slightly, but didn't alter the hot, hungry expression in his eyes. His voice dropped to a low, sexy rasp as he explained. 'I didn't sleep last night because I was thinking about you, and this morning I come out to cool down and here you are. Do you believe in fate...?'

Lily discovered she believed in everything he said in that sinfully sexy voice of his—which probably made her certifiable. 'I really should be going...' *This is pure physical attraction and not a good thing to act on,* she told herself firmly. 'It takes simply ages to dry my hair; it's so thick—'

His authoritative voice cut slickly through her garbled flow of inanity. 'Your hair is rich and lustrous.' He let the damp strands fall through his fingers.

'You think…?' she echoed weakly.

'I do.'

Lily fought to inject a sliver of sanity into the proceedings and shook her head. 'No, it's mousy.' His incredibly long ebony lashes had golden tips and the fine lines that radiated from around his eyes were incredibly attractive.

'We really are going to have to work on that self-esteem issue.'

'We? There is no we. We can't have this conversation. It isn't…*I don't know you*!' Her voice rose in weak protest as her defences went into meltdown.

'What has that got to do with anything?'

'Everything,' she replied, staring helplessly up into his incredible eyes.

He shook his head. 'It is totally irrelevant. Can you deny this feels amazingly *right*?' he challenged as he took her by the shoulders. 'I can't look at you without wanting to sink into your sweet satiny softness and lose myself.'

'You can't say things like to me!' she gasped while thinking, *You can do just anything to me! Please do it now!*

His earthy laugh made every downy hair on her body stand on end. Either he had meant it, or he was a spectacularly good liar! By that point Lily didn't care which it was; she was burning up from the inside out with need.

His shoulders lifted expressively. 'But I just did.' His smile was a potent mix of tenderness and predatory ferocity.

He didn't make any move to stop her when Lily, unable

to resist temptation any longer, reached up and touched his lean cheek. 'I want to see you, touch you.'

His eyes didn't leave hers for a second as he took her fingers from his face and raised them to his lips.

'And you shall,' he promised. 'If that is what you want?'

Lily shook her head. 'I think…I don't know…'

Santiago turned her hand over and traced a path across her palm with the pad of his thumb before touching the plain wedding band on her finger. His head lifted. 'But you are thinking about your husband?'

CHAPTER FOUR

I'M NOT thinking about him, but I should be.

Sucking in a mortified breath, Lily snatched her hand away. His question hadn't just spoiled the mood, it had killed it stone-dead. And a good thing too, she told herself. Her marriage might be a total sham, but she was still married, and in Lily's mind, despite yesterday's reckless thoughts of revenge, Gordon's repeated infidelities didn't give her a licence to do the same.

If she had stopped to think about it, which she hadn't, she would have assumed that Santiago hadn't cottoned on to the fact she was married.

Easy to see how that could happen. She'd been partnerless when he'd seen her, and, unlike women, most men didn't seem to notice things like a wedding band.

It now seemed that he had known she was married all along, and the fact nothing in his manner suggested he had a problem with it made Lily feel totally disgusted.

Not that she was in any position to condemn him. She hadn't exactly run screaming for the hills, had she?

'You shouldn't feel bad.'

Bad! She deserved to feel wretched. 'I wouldn't expect *you* to understand,' she choked contemptuously. Obviously he wouldn't recognise a moral if someone gave it to him gift-wrapped.

A really stomach-churning possibility occurred to her. Had he zeroed in on her *because* she was married? Lily knew there were some men out there, generally commitment phobics, who targeted married women because they

37

didn't want things to get serious. A married woman had clear advantages for that type of sleaze bag.

'I do understand, and what you are feeling is natural,' he soothed.

The compassion in his manner increased Lily's growing anger.

'Done this sort of thing a lot, have you?' She caught her lower lip between her teeth and turned her head away. Angrily she shrugged off the hand that he put lightly on her arm.

'I have handled this badly,' she heard him observe heavily.

Lily's chin lifted. 'So sorry things didn't turn out the way you planned,' she retorted bitterly.

Santiago studied her face before gravely observing, 'It is natural to feel a degree of guilt, a sense that you are being unfaithful—' Lily goggled incredulously at him; this man had to be the most insensitive '—to your husband's memory. I respect you for the way you feel, I really do. In an age when so many place very little value on their marriage vows, your devotion is admirable.'

There was a short time delay before her brain computed what he had said and arrived at the unlikely conclusion— somehow he had the bizarre idea that she was widowed.

Oh, Lord! It should be fun explaining to someone who thought she was a faithful, devoted, grieving widow that her husband was alive and well, and her devotion was the sort that vanished at the first sniff of temptation.

'But you are alive, *querida*, and you are a passionate beautiful woman, with your life ahead of you.' He took her face between his hands. 'I'm sure your husband would have wanted you to be happy. And though I'm sure you won't believe me, one day,' he prophesied confidently, 'you will love again. And until then…'

'Until then…?'

His hands fell away. 'Until then you have needs… appetites…'

'That's where you come in?' Why was she feeling so let down? He was hardly going to tell her that he wanted anything other than to take her to bed. At least he was honest.

'You're not going to deny the attraction between us exists.'

Lily shook her head and wondered what he'd say if she admitted she had never felt anything that even came close to this before.

'Do not let being hurt once make you afraid to live.'

'I'm not,' she said, and realised that for the first time in a long time—perhaps ever—this was true. She took a deep breath; it was time to put him straight. 'As for Gordon, you've got that all wrong. I'm actually totally furious with him.'

'I believe it is not uncommon to feel angry with a loved one who dies. You blame them for leaving you.'

Eyes closed, Lily gave a frustrated sigh and let her head fall back. *I tried, I really tried, and what do I get? Understanding and amateur psychology!*

'No, my husband isn't—'

A nerve clenched in Santiago's lean cheek as he cut across her. 'We keep those we love in our hearts, but there comes a time when we must let go.'

Lily, who would have preferred to put Gordon in a damp, dark, rat-filled cellar, not her heart, stared up at him, her eyes scrunched up in concentration as she tried to figure out how on earth he could have got the idea she was a widow.

'What made you think that my husband is dead?'

'Everyone knows.'

'*People* know?' Oh, heavens, that explained some of the

sympathetic looks she'd been getting. They all had her down as a brave, plucky widow on some sort of romantic pilgrimage!

And here was me thinking how lovely and friendly every-one was.

He nodded. 'I know hotels are meant to be anonymous, but a woman alone in the honeymoon suite is a subject of conjecture. The staff knew the booking was made by your husband, so obviously when you turned up without him they speculated.'

'You'd think they'd have something better to do,' she snapped.

'And then you told Javier...'

'I didn't tell *Javier* anything; I don't know any *Javier*.' She stopped. *'Oh, no!'* Her questioning eyes flew to his face. 'Do you mean the boy at Reception...?'

'The "boy" has a three-year-old son, but, yes, he works Reception sometimes. He's actually a trainee manager.'

Lily wasn't really listening to his explanation; she was recalling arriving back from Baeza and going to pick up her room key. The details, due to the after-effects of the wine, were a bit hazy, but she *could* remember the chap behind Reception looking embarrassed when tears sprang to her eyes after he asked when her husband would be joining her.

'He won't be joining me.' The realisation hit her. *He never intended to.* 'He's gone. He's *really* gone for good.'

Lily absently massaged the tight skin around her temples. One problem solved—she now knew the why. She only had now to figure out how to tell him her husband was alive and well and therefore she was not available.

'Have breakfast with me?'

'What?'

'Breakfast. Not here, if that's what's bothering you. I

know a place about half an hour's drive away. You need a four-wheel drive to get there,' he admitted, 'but, believe me, it is worth it. The setting is superb,' he enthused. 'The food is not fancy, but it's made with fresh local produce and beautifully cooked. Luis has a huge wood-burning oven outside and you can eat alfresco.'

He seemed to take her silence as assent, because he said, 'I'll see you outside in, what…twenty minutes…?' He smiled at her and then dived cleanly into the water.

'You're allowed to be upset, you know.'

'What…?' It took several seconds for Lily to drag her wandering thoughts back to the present and away from the man who had ultimately told her to go to hell.

Well, he got his wish.

Though, of course, she was post-hell now. She'd come out the other side, but would things ever get back to normal? She sometimes wondered if this was normal for her now; maybe she would carry this awful empty feeling around with her for ever…?

'I said you're allowed to be upset.'

A frown formed on Rachel's crease-free forehead. 'Are you coming down with something? You look awfully flushed.'

'No, I'm fine,' Lily lied. 'It's just warmed up this afternoon—' she gestured towards the sun shining through the open window '—and this sweater is a bit—'

'Of a disaster,' Rachel completed. 'I don't mean to be brutal, but this bag-lady look doesn't do you any favours, love.'

'This is casual.'

'No,' Rachel denied brutally, 'it is absolutely awful. Perhaps if you made a bit of an effort you might feel a bit better? If I'm down I buy a pair of shoes…'

'Retail therapy isn't the answer to everything.'

'I didn't mean to be terminally shallow,' Rachel, who had flushed, retorted.

'Of course you're not shallow,' Lily soothed, guilty for being snappy.

'I do actually know a new pair of shoes isn't going to fix everything, but it… Dear God, Lily, if you don't have the right to fall apart after what has happened to you, who does? I tell you, if I'd been through what you have, losing the baby and Gordon, the total scumbag running off with that little—'

Lily did not want to talk about Gordon or his girlfriend, or the baby…especially the baby. 'Am I falling apart?'

'Ever so slightly maybe… Don't you hate Gordon?' Rachel turned her curious gaze on her friend. 'If it was me I'd want to—'

'Maybe I could do with a trim,' Lily interrupted, running a hand lightly over her hair.

'And a new pair of shoes?'

Lily grinned. 'Don't push it, Rachel.' Her grin faded and she hesitantly added, 'About Gordon—you know, he's really not the bad guy in this.'

Rachel looked ready to explode. *Not the bad guy!'*

'And Olivia isn't little.' An image of the athletic red-headed figure of the sports psychologist her ex-husband planned to marry now their divorce was finalised flashed into her head.

'She's six feet in her bare feet and it was hardly a shock when Gordon asked for a divorce.'

Gordon had met her at the airport at the end of her Spanish holiday and Lily, who had been consumed with guilt and more miserable than she had thought possible, had not noticed at first that her husband had been acting oddly. She'd totally forgotten that he had a lot of explaining to do, because so had she.

He had waited until they'd got in the car to admit to her that it hadn't been work that had stopped him joining her, but another woman.

Lily hadn't bothered pretending to be shocked.

'She's called Olivia and she's…well, the thing is, Lily, I want to be with her. I think we should get a divorce.'

'All right.'

Gordon, who had obviously been geared up for a big scene, was gobsmacked by her reaction and slightly suspicious.

'And you don't have a problem with that?'

She shook her head listlessly.

'Don't you want to know…' he flushed '…how long…?'

'If you want to tell me.'

'You do understand what I'm saying, Lily?' He spoke slowly as though he were talking to a child. 'This isn't a fling.'

'Not this time.'

Gordon flushed, and looked defensive. 'Well, if you had been more…' He stopped and made a visible effort to control himself.

She decided to move this along a bit. 'Will there be any fallout…career-wise?'

'I resigned.'

'What about the promotion?' The promotion that was all he'd been able to talk about all year.

A hint of defiance crept into her husband's voice. 'I realised that the civil service was stifling me. I need a change of direction.'

'When did you decide this?'

'I resigned two months ago.'

'Should I ask what you've been doing every morning

when you went off to work…and on those business trips…?'

'Olivia and I are setting up a sports training facility in Cyprus.'

'That's different.' She didn't have to pretend total lack of interest.

'Hell, I didn't mean for it to happen, Lily, but you have to admit we're not…but I don't expect you to understand! The moment I saw her…' he began in a low, impassioned voice.

Lily gazed through the car window not seeing the traffic streaming past. 'Maybe I do understand.'

Gordon didn't say so, but she could see he didn't believe her. For a split second she was tempted to tell him that she had met someone too, and she now knew just how empty their marriage had been. She now knew that love could make a person buy very naughty underwear, and forget every principle she'd been brought up to believe in.

But there was no point. This was Gordon, who had once said comfortingly, 'Of course you're not frigid, you're just not a very *physical* person. Don't worry about it; not everyone is.'

The fact was Gordon thought she was a white-cotton girl. Santiago had made her feel and act like naughty black lace.

Rachel made a scornful sound in her throat. 'Sure it wasn't a shock—you expected your husband to leave you for his bit on the side when you were pregnant.'

Lily pushed her brown hair, which, without its normal monthly trim, had got long and uncontrollable, behind her ears. *Maybe it is time to set the record straight?*

'It's true.' A light flush appeared along the smooth contours of her pale cheeks as she experienced an emotion close to relief as she admitted, 'I really wasn't surprised.

Our marriage had been dead and buried for a long time before Olivia came along.'

Rachel's jaw dropped, but almost immediately she began to shake her head. 'I don't believe it. You two were the couple everyone I know wanted to be.'

Lily looked away. That had been the irony, of course; they had appeared the perfect couple in public. 'It's true,' she said.

'Nobody's *that* good at pretending,' Rachel rebutted. 'I don't how many times I told people that you two proved marriage could work. I mean, you were practically childhood sweethearts.'

Lily ran her tongue over her lips... *When did I last wear lipstick? When did I last wear make-up...?* Rachel was right—it was time she entered the human race again. 'In public, yes.'

There was silence before Rachel sank weakly into the nearest chair. 'So you and Gordon weren't happy? *Seriously...?*'

'I wasn't *unhappy.*'

Rachel folded her long legs underneath her and sighed. 'I don't mind telling you, you've really thrown me, Lily.' Lily lifted her head. 'I never had the slightest hint that things were that bad...or bad at all, for that matter. Why didn't you ever say anything?'

Lily's wide mouth twisted into a bitter smile. 'You make your bed and lie in it—that's what Gran would have said.'

'I'm not your gran, and I know you shouldn't speak ill of the dead but she really was one cold—'

'Leave it, Rachel,' Lily begged.

Rachel acceded with a shrug. 'If you were unhappy, why did you stay, Lily?'

'I thought we might sort things...' Lily stopped and shook her head. 'It's a question I've asked myself a million times. The truth is I don't know why I stayed. Maybe I was lazy, or simply scared of change? Maybe I didn't want to admit I had made a mistake? Perhaps,' she speculated dully, 'a bit of all three.'

'But I never heard you exchange a cross word.' A still-sceptical Rachel gave a mystified frown.

'There were cross words,' Lily admitted, recalling the constant sniping and recriminations. 'But we were past that. The fact is, I think we were both too apathetic to argue by the end.'

'That's so sad.'

Lily, whose own throat closed over with emotion, could only silently echo the sentiment. 'I suppose we were a classic case of two people who grew apart, not together.'

A stunned Rachel exhaled a gusty sigh and shook her head, visibly struggling to come to terms with these calmly voiced revelations.

'I knew straight off that Olivia wasn't like the others.'

It wasn't until the designer bag Rachel had been reaching into to switch off her phone dropped from her nerveless fingers, the contents spilling unheeded over the floor, that Lily realised that she had voiced her thought out loud.

'"The others…!" Gordon had *affairs*?'

Lily met her friend's dazed eyes and admitted awkwardly, 'Two that I know of. There might have been more,' she added in an abstracted voice. *Almost certainly were.*

Rachel released a hoarse laugh. *'I don't believe any of this!'* She shook her head as if to focus her thoughts. 'And you knew…?'

Lily nodded.

'Did you care?'

The flash of her blue eyes lent animation to Lily's pale face. 'Of course I damned well cared!' It had been deeply humiliating, but Gordon had always been filled with remorse afterwards... *They mean nothing to me, Lily.*

Rachel grimaced. '*Sorry.* I still can't believe that you never said a word.' Rachel shook her head in disbelief. 'I'm your best friend.'

Lily's hands lifted in a fluttery, helpless gesture. 'It felt disloyal to talk about it and Gordon begged me not to tell anyone. Can you imagine what Gran would have said if she'd found out, and after she had loaned him the money for that car...?' She stopped and angled a questioning glance at her best friend. 'I suppose this sounds big-time weird to you?'

Rachel didn't deny it. 'And then some!'

'And you think I'm totally pathetic?'

'Well, it's not as if there were children and—' She broke off, a stricken look of horror written on her fair-skinned face. She leapt out of the chair and perched herself on the arm of the chair the other girl occupied. 'Oh, Lily, I'm so, *so* sorry.'

Lily shook her head and smiled reassuringly. 'No, you're right, there weren't.'

'But you couldn't have completely given up the marriage; you tried for a baby?'

Lily fixed her cornflower-blue eyes on her friend's face and shook her head. 'No, we didn't.'

'So it was an accident.' Something that Rachel couldn't identify flickered at the back of Lily's eyes. 'I'm not saying you weren't pleased,' she amended hastily. Nobody who had seen Lily in those early months could have failed to see she was delighted at the prospect of becoming a mother.

'It's the happiest I've ever been,' Lily admitted.

'Well, I don't care what you say, I think he's a total bastard to leave you when you were pregnant.'

'I hadn't slept with Gordon for almost a year before I got pregnant.'

CHAPTER FIVE

THE silence that followed this barely audible announcement stretched until, finally unable to bear it, Lily begged, *'Say something.'*

'You and Gordon…you mean Gordon wasn't the father!'

'Obviously not.' Lily, her eyes closed, passed a hand across her face. She was unable to meet her friend's eyes. 'Nothing you can say could make me feel more wretchedly ashamed than I already do,' she choked.

'What I'm going to say… Oh, Lily, you don't really think I'd pass judgement, do you?'

Lily heard the hurt in her friend's voice and her head came up. 'I wouldn't blame you if you did,' she said miserably. She began to rise, but had not managed to get to her feet before Rachel grabbed her by the shoulders.

'You can't drop a bombshell like that and walk away, Lily,' she protested, still looking totally gobsmacked. 'I want to know everything.'

'There's nothing to know.'

'Nothing! You had an affair. You got pregnant. *You*, of all people. That's *not nothing* in my book. I can't believe that all this time you didn't say a word,' she reproached. 'Who…?' Her eyes widened. 'Are you still seeing him?'

Lily involuntarily inhaled as Santiago's dark, classically featured face appeared in her head.

'Do I know him?'

The words dragged Lily back to the present; she willed herself not to glance towards the open newspaper. 'No, and I'm not still seeing him.'

She didn't add that she was pretty sure he'd cut her dead if he ever did see her, not that that was likely considering the different worlds they lived in.

If things had gone differently she supposed they would have had to meet…? A man had a right to know if he was a father. Very conscious of the leaden weight of misery in her chest, she wondered what his reaction might have been if the baby had survived, and she had told him.

It was possible he might not have wanted to have anything to do with a child conceived by accident, but if he had she supposed they would have had to hammer out some sort of arrangement. Now, though, the speculation was pointless; she'd never know, and neither would he.

'It was a holiday romance, that was all, a fling…' She took a deep breath. 'It meant nothing.' She'd told so many lies and half-truths that another one couldn't matter and if she said it often enough she might even start believing it.

Rachel, her expression serious, studied her friend's pale face, pretty sure the spooky composure she was projecting went only skin-deep. 'When did you meet him?'

'You remember that second honeymoon Gordon and I were meant to have just before he dropped the Olivia bomb on me?'

'The one in that gorgeous hotel in Spain? Didn't Gordon…?'

'Get a call at the airport…yes, that's the one,' Lily confirmed grimly. 'He told me to fly out without him and promised he'd catch a flight the next day. He didn't, and I was pretty mad.'

'Is he Spanish?'

Lily's lips quivered. 'Extremely,' she said drily.

Rachel refilled her glass. 'So, did he work in the hotel?'

'On a…casual basis,' Lily prevaricated.

'Did he *know* that you were pregnant?'

Lily shook her head. 'No, he didn't.' Her voice cracked and she swallowed.

Rachel's eyes suddenly widened to their fullest extent. 'You did know his name, didn't you? It wasn't a one-night stand after too much vino or anything. You shouldn't feel bad. We've all been there done that, and those Spanish waiters can be pretty…well, *pretty.*'

Santiago *a waiter*…! Lily swallowed a bubble of hysterical laughter that lodged in her throat. 'I've not been there done that.'

'No, I don't suppose you have—comes of being a child bride.'

Rachel went to refill Lily's glass, but she shook her head and covered it with her hand. 'No, thanks, and I was hardly a child.'

'In my book nineteen is a child bride. So, you didn't know your waiter's name?'

'I knew his name, and I wasn't drunk.'

Not on alcohol anyhow, no wine had ever affected her the way being around Santiago had. Around him, she'd felt reckless and totally out of control. Now the things she had said to him seemed like a dream. The recollection of how her inhibitions had deserted her when she'd been in his bed brought a dull flush of colour to her cheeks.

'And,' she added, defiance entering her blue eyes, 'if I had the choice, I'd do it again.'

Rachel's eyes widened in comprehension. 'So this one-night stand wasn't so casual?'

'It was for him,' Lily admitted.

A thoughtful expression settled on Rachel's face as she looked at her friend. 'You loved him…?'

Lily sighed. 'Totally,' she admitted, and started to cry.

*   *   *

'The girls are late,' Dan said, checking his watch for the third time. He turned anxiously to the tall dark figure at his side. 'You know what you have to do?'

'I know.'

'It shouldn't be too hard—just turn on the charm, but not around Rachel,' he warned. 'God,' he said with a laugh. 'I'm really nervous.'

'I'd never have guessed.'

'I've never proposed before, and marriage—well, it's a big step, isn't it?' He took a ring box out of his pocket and stared at it. 'And permanent.'

'Not very often.'

'I don't need cynicism; I need support.'

Santiago looked at the younger man's face. 'No, you need a drink, my friend.'

He found that he needed one too. Not that he shared the prospective bridegroom's nerves, but he was conscious of a certain amount of anticipation.

It had been hard to tell from the snapshot—had Lily changed much…? He'd never forget the moment he first saw her in the village square. His breath quickened at the memory.

Driving through the small town on the motorbike his family had gloomily predicted he would kill himself on one of these days, he had stopped to stretch his legs, recalling the conversation they'd had on the subject before he had left home the previous day.

'You have lovely cars,' his mother protested. 'And you can't attend an important meeting in black leather. Nobody will take you seriously.'

'I will change.'

Grinning, his younger sister, Angel, entered the debate. 'I think he wants to forget he's a paid-up member of the establishment…?'

'No,' his other sister corrected, straight-faced. 'He wants

to feel the wind in his tousled hair? I'm right, aren't I, Santiago?'

'Well, I don't care if he wants to walk on the wild side,' their mother retorted, glaring at her tall son. 'He's driving me into an early grave.'

'I'll be careful, I promise.'

He was smiling at the memory and reaching up to unclip his helmet when he saw her. His smile vanished and a reverent sigh shuddered through his body.

'Madre mia!'

From her pensive, almost other-worldly expression, the girl sitting alone at the café table in the square in Baeza seemed to have no idea whatever that she was attracting an enormous amount of appreciative male attention.

She was wearing an ankle-length floaty dress in white. The dress was modest, but not the body it covered.

Her body, *Dios*…!

Even now, it made his breath grow uneven and his body harden just to think about those lush, gently undulating curves. And if the body from heaven weren't enough, she had been blessed with a rare, flawless complexion, big eyes the colour of the bluest cornflowers and a lush and inviting mouth.

If it had been possible to distil that indefinable aura of seductive promise and innocence that this young woman had in abundance, the queue to purchase it would have been stretched from one end of the continent to the other.

He watched her sip her wine, his heart climbing out of his chest as she leaned forward and in the process revealed the upper slopes of her creamy, smooth breasts.

He didn't have the faintest idea how long he stood there motionless, paralysed with lust like an adolescent, but he didn't move a muscle until she got into a taxi, then without questioning his decision he followed it at a discreet distance.

As the taxi turned onto a road that led to only one place, he knew where she was heading.

The first time he had driven along this road it had led to a ramshackle old *finca* and a collection of equally tatty outbuildings. Now it led to a five-star luxury hotel complex set in almost a thousand acres' nature reserve for the lucky guests to enjoy.

Santiago had been born with a name that opened doors in financial and social circles, but when he had approached potential investors to raise money to develop the place he had never once used that name. Stubborn pride…? *Possibly.* A desire to show his father that he wasn't the hopeless loser he frequently painted him as…? *Almost certainly.*

Somewhere along the way to transforming the place into a viable and very successful business, Santiago had realised he was no longer doing it just to prove a point to his father; he was doing it because it gave him a buzz.

He dismounted on exactly the same spot he had ten years earlier, and as he watched the taxi draw up on the forecourt and a shapely female figure emerge he felt no less determined and focused than he had on that first occasion.

Her destination had fitted in with the whole cosmic fate thing he'd had going on in his head. Now he realised he had been rationalising nothing more mystic than lust. Now he knew that it had been a far more malevolent force that had thrown him into the path of Lily Greer.

'It was that turn there.' Rachel bounced up and down in the passenger seat as they passed the pretty village church—for the fourth time.

'Are you sure?' Lily queried.

Rachel looked hurt. 'Of course I'm sure. Don't you think I know what I'm doing?'

Lily sighed and waited for a tractor to pass before she began to back down the narrow village street. 'I'd feel *surer* if you didn't have that map on the wrong page and we hadn't driven round in ever-decreasing circles for the last hour.'

'Don't blame me. It's these instructions Dan gave me; they're impossible. Of course, if he didn't have his phone switched off I could have rung him. Why are you stopping?' she asked as Lily switched the engine off.

'I'm going to ask someone the way.' Over the churchyard wall she had spotted a fair head. 'Give those directions to me and I'll go ask.'

Five minutes later she returned. Rachel was tapping her red-painted nails on the dashboard of Lily's ancient Beetle. 'You took your time,' she complained as Lily slipped back into the driver's seat.

'Sorry, I got talking.'

'Talking? Who to?'

'The vicar. You were right, it's that lane and then the next right and about a mile down there.'

'I knew I was right.'

Lily's brows lifted. 'Well, I suppose according to the law of averages it had to happen some time,' she conceded drily.

'Very funny. If we'd taken my car at least we'd have got lost in comfort,' Rachel said, easing her spine into a more comfortable position in the cramped seat.

'Ah!' Lily gave a triumphant grin. 'So you finally admit we were lost, then?'

'Don't be such a grump. At least we got to see some of this lovely countryside.' Rachel closed her eyes as Lily negotiated a sharp bend. 'What do we do if someone comes the other way?'

Lily, whose thoughts had been running along similar lines, tried to look confident. 'Well, whatever we do it'll be easier than it would be in that monster you drive.'

Fortunately they didn't meet another car and a few minutes later Lily drew up outside a thatched-roof cottage that was picture-postcard pretty. It even had roses around the door.

'Well, isn't this worth it?'

Lily didn't immediately respond. A small paddock divided the cottage from an area of woodland and she had spotted two figures emerge from the tree-lined perimeter. One of them was Dan.

Rachel began to wave her arms. 'There they are!' she cried, catching sight of the men.

'Please tell me that doesn't mean what I think it does,' Lily begged grimly.

Rachel adopted an attitude of surprise and unlatched the garden gate. 'Why? Didn't I say Dan had a friend staying too?'

'Oh, it must have slipped your mind,' grunted Lily sarcastically as she followed her friend through into the garden with considerably less enthusiasm.

'You'll like him,' Rachel slung over her shoulder.

Lily scowled back; she had no intention of liking anyone. 'You're a manipulative monster.'

'Smile,' said Rachel, 'or you'll scare him.' The two men were closer now, so she dropped her voice slightly as she added wistfully, 'Isn't Dan lovely?'

'You're so transparent!' Lily informed her behind a fixed fake smile.

Rachel carried on waving and Lily wondered rather resentfully why her friend could emerge from the tedious journey looking as fresh as a spring morning and she felt—and no doubt looked—as though she'd just been dragged through the proverbial hedge backwards, forwards and sideways!

'For goodness' sake, Lily, *relax.*'

'Relax!' she exclaimed indignantly. 'You've set me up.'

Her friend didn't deny the accusation.

'What is it about people when they get paired off?' Lily grumbled. 'I've told you I'm happy being by myself.'

Briefly the laughter died from the tall blonde's face. 'You're afraid, Lily, and after what you've been through I don't blame you.'

Lily's chin went up. 'I am *not* afraid,' she retorted indignantly. 'I'm cautious.'

'Afraid,' Rachel insisted, kindly, but firmly.

'And I'm not interested.' Lily, who knew she sounded sulky and childish, did her best to ignore her friend's look of hurt reproach. Of course she knew that Rachel *meant* well, and normally she would have accepted her efforts with a smile, but she simply wasn't up to being a *good sport* at that moment.

'You're going to have to take a risk some time, you know.'

That's all you know, thought Lily. She was going all out to have a boring and predictable life from now on. She had had enough of impulses to last her several lifetimes.

'So now you want me to jump into bed with a total stranger.' *Been there done that and look where it got me!*

CHAPTER SIX

'DON'T be ridiculous, Lily. The jumping into bed is totally optional,' Rachel returned, straight-faced.

Lily grinned despite herself.

'What does he look like?' Rachel asked curiously, craning her neck to see beyond a hedge that briefly blocked the two men from view.

'I can't see through a bush,' snapped Lily. The frown between her eyebrows deepened as she added. '''What does he look like?'' Does that mean you don't know?'

'I've never met him, though Dan's always banging on about his wealthy friend.'

'I thought Dan was well off.'

'He is, but this guy has *serious* money, apparently.'

'And like most seriously loaded men probably a taste for tall, skinny blondes with surgically enhanced boobs.' *Great, just when I thought I couldn't be more humiliated.*

'I suppose *you've* known *hundreds* of seriously loaded men…?'

Only one.

'Let me spell out the facts of life. All men have the same fantasies; the rich ones can indulge them—that's the only difference. And I am no man's fantasy.' *One man had convinced her that she was his once.*

'But you're cynical. I don't know about this guy's fantasies, but relax. Dan says he's a…' her freshly glossed lips tugged into a smile '…I think ''top bloke'' were his actual words. Dan knows him through family—their cousins married or something like that.'

'I'm not worrying; I'm going home.'

Rachel shot her friend a look of amused impatience. 'I'm not asking you to marry the man; he's just a bit of male company for the weekend.'

Despite her professed lack of interest, Lily's glance did slide towards the tall—*very* tall—figure who was just emerging from behind the beech hedge. She felt a spasm of sympathy. Was he a fellow victim or willing pawn? Had he been as much in the dark as her?

Once out into the open Dan broke into a run. A moment later he reached them. Lily looked the other way while the reunited couple kissed as though they had been parted for a year, not a few days.

'Well, what do you think of it?' asked the proud owner of the cottage when they came up for air. He slipped an arm around Rachel's waist and hugged her to his side.

'It's perfect!' Rachel declared as she snuggled up kitten-like to him.

'Not as perfect as you, darling.'

Oh, please! thought Lily as she averted her gaze for the second time. Rachel suddenly grabbed her shoulder.

'Don't look now,' she whispered.

Naturally, Lily immediately wanted to do just that. 'What is it?'

'Not what, *who*,' Rachel corrected. 'Your date is my dream man—no offence, darling,' she slung hurriedly over her shoulder to an amused-looking Dan. 'How do you feel about swopping…?' Her eyebrows lifted. 'You have Hugh Grant, I get Antonio Banderas.'

'I look nothing whatever like Hugh Grant,' Dan protested.

'I've no idea what you're talking about.' Lily shook her head, laughing.

'You will,' Rachel promised. *'Oh, wow!'* She raised her voice. 'Well, hello there. I'm Rachel.'

Unable to restrain herself any longer, Lily turned around; the half-smile on her lips froze where it was.

Rachel's nonsense now made sense. Nothing much else did! Lily took it all in in the blink of an eye: the mobile, sensual mouth, the strong, hawkish nose, the slanted ebony brows.

During that time she drank in the details her heart stopped; it stopped dead. When it started up again she took several long, gulping gasps to pull some oxygen into her depleted lungs. She could literally feel the blood drain from her face.

'Hello, Rachel,' said Santiago, dressed informally but expensively in faded designer jeans that clung to his long, muscular thighs, a linen shirt that hung open to reveal a black tee shirt underneath. Against the dark cotton his skin had the sheen of dull gold.

'This is Lily.' It seemed to Lily that Rachel's voice came from a long way away.

This isn't happening, thought Lily. She looked up into dark, deep-set glittering eyes. This was a man with eyes that could make a girl forget that she was *nice*, eyes that could make a girl feel like a woman.

'Say hello, Lily.'

She would have taken to her heels right then, regardless of any lingering impression she might have left of lunacy, if a creeping paralysis hadn't nailed her feet to the spot. Despite the glorious hot summer weather and the inappropriately heavy clothing she wore, she felt herself grow icily cold and clammy.

Santiago was not a man who did things by halves; when he loved it was full-on, mind-blowing love...the sort of love that... She sucked in air through her flared nostrils.

Do not go there, Lily. Do not go anywhere near there!
When he hated it was with equal fervour. And he hated her!

She thought about the expression on his face in Spain when he had personally delivered a message. *Your husband rang Reception. He says he is worried because your phone is switched off, and could you please contact him?*

He really hated her.

Santiago Morais could not be here, but he was! And she was looking at him. Could there be two men who looked or moved this way?

She already knew the answer to this desperate question.

'Hello.'

His dark head moved slightly in acknowledgement of her croaky greeting. Briefly their eyes connected, and there was absolutely no recognition whatsoever in those dark, enigmatic depths.

His head dipped slightly. 'Hello.'

She *felt* different from the woman he had known a year ago. She knew she looked different, and, she was willing to admit, not in a good way, but surely she hadn't changed that much?

What did you want? she asked herself. A big scene? No, but an acknowledgement they had met would have been nice. Well, maybe nice wasn't the right word, she privately conceded. But it would have been, well, better than *this*. Was this his way of telling her that as far as he was concerned she or, rather, *they* had never happened?

Colour, hot and uncomfortable, came flooding back into her face; the first stirring of protest wakened in her tight chest. Blighting contempt, outright animosity would have been easier to take than being disregarded.

'Rachel, this is Santiago Morais, my sort-of cousin.' Dan

grinned. 'This man gave me a job when nobody else would.'

'I always was a risk-taker.'

'I thought you were just a good judge of character,' Dan retorted.

The dark, heavy-lidded eyes she still dreamt about skimmed over Lily once more; this time anger slipped past his impassive mask. 'So did I,' he said enigmatically.

Lily caught her quivering lower lip between her teeth. She was denied the comfort of weeping, and for a brief vulnerable moment shimmering hurt was reflected in the swimming blue depths of her eyes.

'Well, I always follow my instincts,' Rachel announced.

'And are your instincts always right?' Santiago asked her.

Rachel looked rueful. 'Unfortunately not,' she admitted.

Santiago smiled at her. Having once been on the receiving end of that smile, Lily understood Rachel's dazed expression. Santiago had a way of smiling that made the recipient feel special.

For a short time Lily had thought she was that special person; now she recognised the smile for what it was: a cynical manipulation.

'Dan has talked non-stop about you, Rachel, and I'm glad to report that none of it was exaggeration—you do look like a summer's day.'

Lily watched the delight spread across her friend's face and felt the most shameful stab of jealousy lance through her.

'Did you say that, darling?'

'I would have if I'd thought about it. I've not the way with words that Santiago has.'

'You don't do so badly, sweetheart.'

'Did you have a good journey?'

Lily's jaw tightened as she felt her control begin to un-ravel. 'Not particularly.'

The response drew the fleeting brush of Santiago's dark eyes and Rachel's laughing rebuke. 'Lily got cranky be-cause she got us lost,' she teased.

'I didn't get lost.' She spoke automatically, her feverish thoughts occupied elsewhere. Had Santiago known she would be here? That made no sense because, considering how they had parted, it seemed unlikely, bordering remote, that he would actively seek her out.

This had to be some sort of ghastly coincidence.

'The lack of signposts are part of the charm of the place,' Dan claimed. 'And that smell.' He inhaled deeply. 'You get nothing like this in the city,' he said, and then started coughing.

A laughing Rachel patted him on the back. 'The air is like champagne, darling, but I can't wait to see the house.'

Lily supposed a conversation of some sort must have occurred, she might even have participated in it, but the next thing she had any real recollection of was being inside the cottage.

Rachel went around the room exclaiming at the quaint-ness of it all. She loved it.

'The sound system is concealed in the dresser,' the cot-tage owner boasted, indicating a dark oak Welsh dresser.

And what's a country cottage without surround sound? Lily thought, leaning heavily on the arm of a leather arm-chair. The interior of the low-beamed room had been painted white; so, for that matter, had the beams. It was furnished minimally with modern expensive pieces that made no concessions to the age of the building.

'I gutted the place,' she heard Dan unnecessarily an-nounce. 'I wanted light and space, like a loft apartment.'

Dan's interior-design efforts hadn't made the low ceilings higher. In the periphery of Lily's vision she was conscious of Santiago ducking to avoid a low beam as he stepped into the room. She forced herself to breathe more slowly as the feelings of claustrophobia intensified.

Santiago moved with the fluid grace only he was capable of and positioned himself in front of what had once been a fireplace and was now a hole in the wall. 'You already have a loft apartment.'

Dan took his friend's dry comment as a joke and laughed. 'Would you ladies like to see your rooms? Then afterwards I'll give the guided tour of the garden. I've got the barbecue going…well, almost,' Dan added with a grin.

'Great. There's nothing we like more than burnt meat, is there, Lily?'

Not unless that something was being underneath a warm, hard, satin-skinned man who told you you were beautiful, who told you that you drove him crazy and then did the same to you…again and again…

'Love barbecues,' said Lily thickly, her breath coming a little faster as she stared at the wooden floor as though it were the most fascinating thing she'd ever seen. 'Hard wood?' she added brightly as she rubbed her toe along the polished surface.

Dan was happy to supply the information. 'Reclaimed from a local chapel that was being demolished.'

'Yes, but what have you done to the bedroom, darling?' Rachel, who was tired of DIY talk, purred.

Dan grinned. 'Let me show you…?' Rachel laughed huskily. 'We'll be back directly. Santiago will look after you, Lily. Won't you, Santiago?'

Horror swept over Lily at the thought of being 'looked after' by Santiago. Her alarm-filled eyes lifted and connected with Santiago's darkly malicious gaze.

'There's nothing I'd like more,' he agreed smoothly.

'I could really do with the bathroom,' Lily interrupted quickly. She desperately had to get away from him.

Displaying an impressive turn of speed, Lily was already halfway up the steep narrow staircase by the time Dan's 'Second on the right,' reached her. In the bathroom she splashed her face with cold water and tried to recover her composure or, failing that, regain the ability to stop hyper-ventilating.

She had no idea for how long she stood there with cold water playing over her wrists in the washbasin. But her fingers were icily cold by the time she shook them dry and the voices she had been vaguely conscious of had receded and grown faint.

'Tomorrow,' she promised herself. 'I'll leave, and all this will be a bad memory.' She really wanted to go tonight, but she knew that Rachel would be suspicious if she walked out now and she didn't want to ruin her friend's weekend, even if that friend did set her up with strange men.

Only this man wasn't a stranger!

She closed her eyes and took a deep restorative breath. *Come on, Lily, show a bit of backbone,* she chided herself. One evening; how hard could it be…?

Very hard, as it turned out!

CHAPTER SEVEN

THE start was not auspicious.

Lily walked out of the bathroom and found herself standing, not in the small room with a slanted roof and a single bed she had hurriedly identified as her own in her quick dash through to the bathroom, but a larger room with a double bed. She stood for a moment totally disorientated, before she realised that the bathroom must interconnect with the two guest bedrooms.

Her restless gaze took in the black robe slung across the back of a chair, the damp towel crumpled on the bed suggesting that the owner had stepped out of the shower and dropped it there. The scatter of personal items on the dressing table, the elusive male fragrance that hung lightly in the air, told her who slept in that bed.

Her stomach took a deep and unscheduled dip, and the muscles low in her pelvis contracted violently. A hand pressed to her mouth stopped the involuntary cry escaping her lips, but did nothing to quell the smothering excitement that made her treacherous body literally shake.

Santiago the other side of my bathroom door. Now that should really help me sleep! She tried to laugh and found she couldn't; you couldn't make a joke out of something that had all the making of a tragedy.

Every instinct told her she ought to get out of that room as fast as was humanly possible.

So why am I standing here?

She actually started to walk towards the door. She didn't

get there. Something, possibly an untapped streak of masochism, made her linger.

She never could recall the sequence of events that led to her standing there fingering the heavy watch that lay on the bedside table. The heavy metal was smooth and cold in her palm as she turned it over recalling the occasions when she had seen it against his brown flesh.

'The clasp is faulty.'

The observation came from behind her. Lily almost leapt out of her skin at the sound of the deep, sexily accented voice.

A picture of guilt, her cheeks flaming, she spun around jerkily. Her eyes collided with those of the tall figure who stood, his narrow hip wedged against the door-jamb, his arms folded across his chest.

She experienced a surge of adrenaline that made her feel light-headed as she looked at him. Head cocked at an arrogant angle, his eyes narrowed and that marvellous golden skin stretched taut across the angles of his magnificent cheekbones, he looked dark and dangerous and, she couldn't deny it, quite incredibly gorgeous in a fallen-angel sort of way.

One dark brow quirked expressively and Lily realised that she'd been standing there staring at him...for how long she hadn't the faintest idea.

'Did you get lost again?' His expressive, mobile lips set in a straight line of disdain, his narrowed eyes continued to scan her flustered face without warmth.

'Sorry...I d-didn't mean...I thought this was...I was thinking about someone...thing, *something* else.' *I was thinking about you.* 'I thought I was in my own room, but obviously I wasn't.' Her hands moved in a fluttery gesture as she stopped.

The longer his eyes held hers, the less articulate she became, but he didn't help her out. He just carried on staring her down. Lily felt a surge of resentful anger.

'Anyhow, what are you doing here?'

Her aggressive addition caused his eyebrows to lift in an attitude of exaggerated surprise. 'This is my bedroom.'

The dry reminder made her shift uncomfortably and twist her hands in an anguished knot of white-knuckled fingers.

'I know that now.'

'Now that you have gone through the drawers.'

The suggestion brought her chin up. 'I didn't touch the drawers.' Her eyes held a sparkle of resentment as they rested on his dark, disdainful face. 'I wasn't snooping, if that's what you're implying.'

'How exactly would you define entering someone else's bedroom and rifling through their belongings?'

The feverish spots of colour on her cheeks expanded until her entire face glowed with painful colour. 'I didn't *intentionally*... As I said, I didn't even know it was your room.'

The contention drew a nasty smile from him.

Lily gritted her teeth. 'I was just...it takes me a while to get my bearings.' *Especially when I'm in shock!* And seeing Santiago standing there had to qualify as that.

The fragile grip on her panic slipped as she contemplated the night ahead. *Then don't think ahead!* she cautioned herself sternly. *Better still, don't think at all, and say less.*

'Don't worry, it won't happen again.' The first time they had made love she had said the same thing.

But it had!

Something that flickered in the back of his eyes made her wonder if he remembered too. Recalled how rapidly she had retracted and ended up in his bed, and the memory filled her with a deep sense of shame.

Obviously she was no longer that weak, wanton creature.

You hope!

And with her head held stubbornly high, her eyes focused on anything but him, as she began to edge towards the door she realised that to leave the room would mean getting past Santiago. Maybe even brushing against him!

She came to an abrupt halt, and a shudder she had no control over ran visibly through her frame as she contemplated the inevitable physical contact with warm, hard muscle.

'Excuse me…' He didn't respond to her frigidly polite request to move. 'That's a polite way of saying shift out of my way.' Rudeness had an equally poor result. He just stood there looking at her.

'How have you been, Lily?'

She blinked. 'Do you care?'

'You acted as though you were surprised to see me here.'

'I was…' Her eyes narrowed suspiciously. 'If you're suggesting I angled for an invite because I knew you'd be here, nothing could be farther from the truth. If I'd known you'd be here I never would have come,' she promised him. 'My friend invited me. I came, end of story.'

His upper lip curled.

'Do I get to know what the sneer's for?' she asked. Like everything else, Santiago's look of disdain was perfect.

'So this is a happy coincidence…?'

Lily's spine stiffened. 'I'd prefix that with cruel or painful.'

'So your friend didn't mention my name…?'

'I don't think she knew it.'

She continued to grind her teeth quietly; that sceptical smirk of his was off-the-scale aggravating. 'What the hell else could it be if it wasn't a coincidence?'

'I don't know—'

'Amazing, I thought you knew everything,' she cut in childishly.

'Maybe you thought we might start up where we left off?' he suggested sardonically.

Lily tried to sound calm despite the fact she would have liked to take a swing at him. 'We left off with you screaming abuse at me, as I recall.' Her expression was intended to give the impression she found the recollection amusing. The reality was a long way from the truth.

That traumatic encounter was seared into her psyche. And actually he hadn't shouted. When Santiago got mad the volume dropped, and the deep, soft syllables were more devastating than any bellow.

'But,' she added helpfully, 'if you're worried your animal magnetism might prove too much for my control, you can always lock the door this side. And then you can sleep sound in the knowledge that I won't creep into your bed in the middle of the night.'

The moment the scornful words left her lips she knew she had shot herself in the foot. Santiago might have been suitably put in his place by her scathing wit, but she couldn't look at him to find out.

Some wit! Her imagination had gone into overdrive, or, rather, her memory, because imagination wasn't required when you had actually done it!

With a little jerky motion of her head she began to study the blue-striped curtains at the window—the fabric looked expensive. Fabric patterns were a much safer subject than a naked Santiago.

But it wasn't fabric patterns that flooded her head, but forbidden memories. She had woken and been drawn from the warmth of the bed they had shared by the moonlight that had shone through the open balcony window. The air had been thick with the scent of the sea and the heavy fragrance of thyme and lemon trees planted in the terracotta pots around the wrought-iron railings had hung in the air.

Returning to the bed later, she had stood beside it looking at the face of her lover. The strong angles of his face had been softened by sleep. A deluge of emotion so intense that it had brought a hot flood of unshed tears to her eyes had left her feeling breathless and shaky.

So this is love. I always was slow, she thought. *Who else waits until they're twenty-five to fall in love…?*

'Love hurts' had suddenly had an entirely new meaning.

When she'd pulled back the cover and slipped back into the bed beside him she had been cold. For a breathless moment she could literally *feel* the texture of warm satiny skin against her own, as she'd plastered her cold body against his. The tight, congested feeling in her chest became suffocating. It was all so real: the friction of hair-roughened areas against her bare, sensitised flesh, the heat building up between them as pale limbs entwined deliciously with brown.

Lily was too caught up by the unrelenting stream of images passing through her mind to notice that Santiago's response was a long time coming and with his dark skin a flush was easy to miss.

'I'll keep that in mind.'

She gave a dazed blink and focused on his lean face. 'Yeah, well, just remember I've got a lock my side too, and,' she added defiantly, 'I'll be using it.'

His dark eyes moved over her face. 'Have you looked in the mirror recently?'

Not if I can help it. She had no control over the mortified flush that washed over her fair skin, though she managed not to lift a hand to her hair. 'If I'd known you'd be here I'd have had a makeover,' she retorted flippantly.

'It would take more than a makeover.'

Lily, her eyes shocked, froze when he caught hold of her chin between his thumb and forefinger and tilted her face up to him. Head angled back, eyes half closed, long dark lashes brushing his cheek, he scanned her face, then let his hand fall away before delivering his damning verdict.

'You look appalling.'

The verdict tore a shaky laugh from her throat as she absorbed this ego-bashing body-blow. Lily took a step back. 'You always were a smooth talker,' she said, tucking her hair behind her ears with not-quite-steady hands.

'What the hell have you been doing with yourself?'

Lily found the depth of anger in his snarling demand bewildering. Before she had the opportunity to tell him to mind his own business he added sneeringly, 'I hope he was worth it.'

'I'm a slow learner, but I've come to the conclusion that no man is *worth it*.'

Santiago didn't appear to be listening to her. A distracted expression slid across his face as he extended a brown hand towards her. 'Your skin is still smooth.'

A sibilant little gasp snagged in her throat as his thumb began to travel from the curve of her jaw up her cheek. From somewhere she discovered the strength to pull away. Blindly she barged past him and stumbled towards the door.

She almost made it, but her shoulder caught the sharp corner of a tallboy. A cry of pain was wrenched from her lips as half the items from the polished surface went crashing noisily to the floor. Wiping the wetness from her cheeks with the back of her hand, she dropped down and began to agitatedly gather the things that had fallen on the polished boards.

Above her Santiago swore fluently in his native tongue. 'Be careful; there's broken glass.'

'It's fine,' she sniffed.

Santiago dropped down beside her. 'You're bleeding.'

Lily kept her head down and ignored his husky observation.

'I said stop that,' he snarled, grabbing hold of her wrist. 'You're bleeding over everything.'

'Sorry.' Lily held her injured hand against her chest. 'I'll pay for any damage.'

'To hell with the damage. Let me see…'

The idea of him touching her again made her heart rate kick up another notch. She would sooner put her hand in a flame than invite his touch. 'It'll be fine; it's just a little cut,' she muttered, not looking at him, but very conscious of how dangerously close he was.

'You should clean it. There could be glass in it,' he said, pulling her to her feet and sounding angry. *So nothing new there.*

'Don't fuss,' she gritted, pulling her elbow out of his supportive grasp.

'Let me see.'

Lily ran the tip of her tongue across her dry lips and flickered a wary look at him through her lashes.

'There's no need to make a production of this.'

'Then don't,' he suggested, stony-faced.

'It's a scratch,' she insisted, beginning to clumsily off-load the things she was still holding onto the nearest solid surface, which happened to be his bed.

She grimaced as items from his wallet spilled out untidily over the quilt. Teeth set, she tried to stop them falling on the floor. Her efforts were hampered by the fact she still had one hand pressed against her chest.

'That would suggest otherwise.'

She followed the direction of his finger and saw the red stain spreading across her pale sweater. 'Damn!' she exclaimed, grimacing. 'I'd better change.'

'That would be a good idea. Dan faints at the sight of blood,' Santiago told her drily. 'But *after* I've looked at it.'

'You haven't changed a bit.' As she levelled her angry glare at his face she wondered if maybe Dan wasn't the only one who didn't like the sight of blood. Santiago looked unusually pale. 'You still have to be in control of everything,' she accused, beginning to rub a spot of blood from a snapshot that had fallen from his wallet.

'You never used to mind that I was hands-on.'

The mortified colour flew to Lily's cheeks. 'That's something I prefer not...' Her voice died away as she straightened up, the photo grasped in her fingers. Her eyes, round and shocked, went from it to him.

'You knew I'd be here.'

Santiago took the stained snapshot from her fingers and gave a careless shrug. 'I barely recognised you.'

'But you did,' she snapped accusingly. 'You *knew* I would be here and you still came and then,' she added, her indignation escalating, 'you accused *me* of trying to get back in your bed!'

'You introduced the subject of beds.'

Forgetting her cut hand, she grabbed his hand in both hands and released a long, low, anguished groan. 'We could have avoided this.' Her bewildered eyes locked with his. 'Why did you come, if you knew I was here, Santiago?'

He didn't respond. 'Have you been ill?'

'We're not all as image-conscious as you are.'

Actually Santiago had many faults, but vanity, she admitted, was not one of them. He didn't work on his image; you had to care about what people thought about to do that. Santiago had a 'take me or leave me' attitude that many people took for arrogance. They might well be right, she reflected grimly.

'That's not an answer,' he pointed out impatiently.

'Maybe I don't think I owe you any explanations. It's pretty obvious that you don't think you owe me any.' She shook her head. 'I still can't imagine what you were thinking of coming here?'

'Maybe I wanted to see how many scalps you had added to your belt since me?'

'Oh, my,' she said airily, 'I've lost count. Rachel and Dan will wonder where we are. We should go down.'

'Perhaps they'll think we succumbed to instant lust and have fallen into bed.'

Lily inhaled and shook her head. 'That's enough.'

'Enough of what?'

'Enough of you acting like I'm something that just crawled out from under a stone. Just what is your problem anyway?'

His head reared back, the muscles in his brown throat worked as he looked down at her with incredulous disdain. 'The fact you can ask that question…'

She expelled the air from her lungs in a long, hissing sigh of weary exasperation. 'I was married and I let you think I wasn't.'

'You played the vulnerable, grieving widow,' he condemned.

'And you were only too eager to take advantage of my vulnerability, as I recall.'

'Do you think I don't know that? Do you think I didn't know that at the time…?' He gave a bitter laugh. 'Do you think I didn't despise myself?'

'And now you just despise me…that must be convenient. Oh,' she sighed sadly. 'I shouldn't have deceived you, I'm aware of that, but it was a year ago and it's not like you were left with any permanent emotional scars or anything. It's just your pride. I suppose it's being Spanish, the macho thing.'

Santiago had been moving as she spoke; now he was standing so close they were almost touching. He didn't touch her, but she wanted him to. This, she thought despairingly, was why history kept repeating itself…the human race was incapable of learning by its mistakes, no matter how painful. Or at least she was!

'You sound quite an authority on the subject.'

She was normally sensitive to intonation, but the heavy irony in his voice sailed over Lily's head as she tried to focus her eyes halfway up his chest. Her eyes had other ideas.

'Well, it was only sex…very good sex,' she added fairly. 'But just sex when all said and done…' *You're gibbering,* she thought and closed her mouth. Her eyes stayed stubbornly, some might say suicidally, focused on the severe sexy line of his incredible mouth.

It was a few seconds later that her fuddled brain registered the anger etched on his lean face.

'You're right, the sex was good.' His voice was like warm honey as he leaned towards her. Their eyes connected and the crackling tension went off the scale.

There was no moisture left in Lily's mouth as she swallowed convulsively. The unique scent of his warm male body filled her nostrils and she felt dizzy. She was not aware of the strangled sound of distress that emerged from her aching throat.

Lily closed her eyes and concentrated all her resources on regaining control. A moment later she opened her eyes and managed a shrug.

'Yes, we had a good time, didn't we?'

'The sort of good time that leaves a nasty taste in the mouth.'

The insult made her flinch, but her chin lifted. 'Well, we

both agree on something, then. Now, if you'll excuse me, I'm going downstairs.'

'Looking like that?'

'Oh!' Lily glanced down at her top and grimaced. 'I'll get changed… Damn, my things are in the car.'

'Never mind your damned clothes, you need that hand cleaned up. Come on.' Ignoring her squeal of protest, he placed both hands on her shoulders and propelled her into the adjoining bathroom. It was a small room, which got a lot smaller with him in it. Lily knew that if she dwelt on the confined space she would start to hyperventilate.

'Right, sit there and let me have a look.'

Perched on the edge of the bath, she glared resentfully at the top of his dark head as he inspected her cut hand.

'It's deep,' he concluded after a moment, 'but I don't think it needs stitches.'

She snatched her hand away. 'Damned right it doesn't.' After the last experience she didn't want to see the inside of a hospital for a long time.

'You're lucky—there doesn't seem to be any glass fragments in it. It needs cleaning and dressing, though.' He switched on the cold-water tap. 'Put it under the water and I'll get something to clean it with.'

'I really don't think—'

'And I really don't care what you think,' he cut in with blighting scorn. 'So shut up and for once in your life do as you're told.'

Lily put her hand under the tap, not because he'd said so, but because she was dripping blood all over the marble tiled floor. 'Mr Charm,' she muttered darkly as he left the room.

A couple of minutes later he returned carrying a bottle of antiseptic, a bandage and several sundry items.

'Where did that come from?'

'The first-aid kit in my car. I told them you'd had an accident. Dan's bringing up your bags.' He dropped down onto his knees at her feet and gestured for her to give him her hand.

Lily did so with reluctance. He was impressively deft and in a matter of moments her wound was cleaned and neatly dressed. After a final inspection he appeared satisfied. His eyes lifted to hers. 'Does that feel comfortable—not too tight?'

She shook her head. 'Thank you.'

'Lily...you asked me why I came knowing—' At the sound of Dan noisily dumping her bags in the adjoining room he broke off. 'You're welcome,' he said, rising to his feet in one fluid motion.

A brief nod and he was gone, leaving Lily to wonder about what he had been going to say.

CHAPTER EIGHT

HAD anyone even noticed when she had excused herself pleading a headache last night? Well, that at least was no lie. Lily pressed her fingers to her temples. This morning the heavy thud from last night had been reduced to the gentle throb of a tension headache. *Me tense…? Now, there's a surprise!*

Her expression sour, she looked at her reflection in the mirror. It was the same image that had looked back at her for weeks, the only difference was this time it shocked her.

I barely recognise myself, she thought, lifting a stubborn hank of hair from her cheek. That at least looked healthy. She let it slide through her fingers, slippery clean and shiny as a conker. Its original cut was a dim and distant memory, but it didn't look too bad.

The same couldn't be said for the rest of her! It wasn't just the fact that she wore no make-up and her clothes had been selected without any concession to style or colour co-ordination. Lily recognised that her body language screamed defeat, the same message was conveyed by the expression in the shadows of her blue eyes.

She was frowning at her frumpy reflection when the sound of laughter drifted up the stairs along with the smell of breakfast. They were having fun; a wave of self-pity washed over her. *Now how daft is that?* she asked herself. *Nobody made you go to bed early. Nobody made you sit in a corner saying nothing all night.* A few inarticulate grunts had been her major contribution to the evening's festivities.

A light of resolution awoke in her wide-spaced eyes and,

purposefully straightening her pathetically hunched shoulders, she stalked to the wardrobe and pulled open the doors.

The contents did not offer much choice. Finally she pulled out a pair of cream linen trousers and a sleeveless, plain, fine-rib black vee-neck sweater that still had the shop label attached. When she pulled them on the trousers were too big for her new slimline self so she substituted them with a butterfly-patterned voile skirt in soft pastel shades.

She chewed her lip for a moment and wondered what to do with her hair, then on impulse she pulled it back in a severe pony-tail high on her head. She secured it with a silk scarf and freed a few long tendrils of soft hair to curl around her face and nape. It had a softening effect and drew attention to the swan-like curve of her slender, pale throat.

'My goodness!' she said aloud to the mirror. 'I've got cheekbones.'

Fascinated by the discovery, she traced the slanting outline, not sharp enough to cut yourself on, but definitely cheekbones. Purposefully, with the occasional glance back at the strange girl in the mirror, she emptied the contents of her bag onto the bed. Sifting through the motley collection of make-up from the bottom of her handbag, all she came up with was a soft apricot gloss, which she applied to her lips then, for good measure, her eyelids and the apples of her cheeks too. The difference the subtle smudges of colour made was amazing.

After breakfast Dan and Rachel announced their intention to walk into the village to buy some milk.

Santiago looked at the spindly high-heeled shoes that the bubbly blonde was wearing and thought about the lane with its numerous potholes. He doubted they would go far. 'Enjoy yourselves,' he said, unfolding the previous day's financial pages.

'We will,' they promised in unison.

He heard the sound of the back door slamming and then seconds later it opening again. 'Forgot my shades,' Dan said in a voice loud enough to reach his girlfriend outside and then, in a lower, confidential tone, he added, 'Listen, Santiago, mate, I'm really sorry about...' With a grimace he jerked his head suggestively upwards. 'My God, was she hard going last night or what?'

'I thought she was a little quiet.' She hadn't laughed once all night. He had liked her laugh. He had made her laugh just to watch her face light up.

'You're being generous,' Dan said, and then wondered at the odd expression that flitted across his friend's face.

'Are you coming or not?' A smiling Rachel popped her blonde head around the door.

Dan smiled. 'Just coming.' He gave a conspiratorial nod towards his friend and made to leave.

'If Lily wakes while we're gone, tell her I won't be long. It's great to see her sleeping late,' she mused. 'I *knew* the country air would do her good,' she confided happily. 'I bet she's glad I persuaded her to come now.'

'Your friend...she has been ill?'

It seemed to Santiago, after considering the alternatives, that illness was the only thing that could explain Lily's altered appearance.

The permanent crease line between his dark brows deepened as he recalled her expression when she had recognised him the previous day. There had been enough shock, pain and desperate hurt in those wide blue eyes to satisfy the most vengeful of ex-lovers.

Wasn't that what he was? Hadn't that been his intention—to see her suffer? Certainly she deserved to. She had done what no other woman ever had; she had made a fool of him. *Though not without my help.*

The truth was it had provided him with no pleasure, no sense of triumph, to see the pinched pain in her face and the shocking dark smudges under her eyes. He supposed it might have if he were the sort of man who got a kick from making a helpless puppy whimper. Damn the woman! Only a sadistic bastard could take revenge, petty or otherwise, on someone who looked as though they had been to hell and back.

So far nothing had gone as planned. He'd had it all worked out, what would happen when he saw her again. He would be able to view her beauty with objectivity, and leave at the end of the weekend wondering what he had ever seen in her. End of story, get on with the rest of his life.

It turned out he had been slightly optimistic about the objectivity part. And he knew *exactly* what he had seen in her.

He had also forgotten to include the unforeseen into his calculations. And he definitely hadn't foreseen feeling a powerful urge to feed her, protect her from cold winds and crush with his bare hands the person responsible for turning a vibrant, glowing woman into a shadow.

'She's had a bad year,' Rachel explained.

Haven't we all? he thought.

'She's a bit…emotionally *delicate* just now.'

And not just emotionally, he thought, recalling the extreme fragility of her wrist bones. They had looked as though a light breeze would snap them, let alone a man holding them—not that he had any intention of holding her or them.

Though it was not immediately obvious because of the bulky outfit she had been wearing, it would seem likely her body had lost its luscious curves. He had woken in the middle of the night on more occasions than he cared to acknowledge with an ache that nothing but holding her soft, fragrant body could assuage.

A man who knew his own weaknesses could guard against them. Last night his guard had come close to slipping. With a frown he pushed aside the intrusive thought.

'Though she looks a million times better than she did a few weeks ago. I don't mind telling you I was really worried…'

A million times better? Madre mia! This information shocked him more than he could say.

Rachel looked as if she might say more, then at the last moment appeared to have second thoughts. With a quick awkward smile over her shoulder, she followed Dan outside.

He smelt Lily before he even heard her soft tread on the flagged passageway. He inhaled the scent of the floral soap she used and the shampoo she washed her hair with.

Lily walked, her feet encased in a pair of silly but pretty sandals, into the kitchen. She stood framed in the doorway blissfully ignorant of the fact the morning sun had made her skirt effectively transparent. When she saw that Santiago was alone she almost turned around.

She took a deep breath and stuck out her chin. 'Good morning.'

His eyes lifted to hers and then dropped as he continued to scan the paper.

Lily entered the room, and when Santiago made no attempt to move his long legs from her path she stepped over them. Clearly her efforts to re-enter the human race were wasted on him. Not that the effort she had made had anything to do with him.

She sat down in a chair opposite him. Arms folded in an

unconsciously protective gesture across her chest, she examined his remote profile.

'Where are Dan and Rachel?'

There was no reply.

'Don't you think this is rather silly?' She sucked in an angry breath and her hands twisted together into a white-knuckled knot as, his dark head turned from her, Santiago continued to scan the page of print.

'I'm talking to you,' she added in an overloud voice that trembled with emotions that threatened to spill over. 'Would a little bit of common courtesy be too much to ask?' she demanded.

The newspaper rustled as he laid it to one side. Very slowly his eyes lifted to hers. 'Frankly, yes.' Though the muscles in his brown throat worked as his eyes meshed with her indignant blue orbs, his expression didn't alter.

'Is that it?' she choked.

'What do you want me to say...?' *You look delicious and I want to take your clothes off.*

The mild question brought a look of confusion to her face. 'I don't want anything from you.'

Santiago appeared to believe that statement about as much as she did. 'Are you annoyed,' he suggested, 'that I have not noticed the trouble you have taken with your appearance this morning?' His dark eyes dropped, moving with slow, insolent deliberation over her slim figure. 'I have.'

Their eyes connected once more and the gleam of predatory heat in Santiago's caused all the muscles in Lily's abdomen to spasm violently. Trying desperately to ignore the flash of suffocating heat that had engulfed her, she lifted her chin in a gesture of empty defiance and swallowed past the dry, tight occlusion in her throat.

'Well, don't think I did it for you.' She shook her head

vigorously and felt her pony-tail bang against her cheek. 'Because I didn't.' *Well, if he wasn't thinking it he sure as hell is now…way to go, Lily!*

'So Dan is the lucky man. Perhaps I should warn your friend.'

Lily tossed her head. *He thinks I'm a conniving tart, why not give the man what he wants?* 'Dan isn't my type, but, naturally,' she added, fabricating an insincere smile out of pure loathing. 'I would steal him from my best friend without a second thought.'

'Then what is your type?'

You are. It made her blood chill to think how close she came to saying it out loud. Her eyes slid from his. 'I have abysmal taste in men,' she confided huskily.

'Is one of these…*men* responsible for your present condition?'

'*Condition…?*' Her voice rose, hoarsely suspicious. Without realising it she pressed her hands to her stomach. 'I'm not pregnant, if that's what you're insinuating.' She might smile about the irony of this conversation later, but at that moment she was fighting back the tears. Anger, she had learnt, was a pretty good way of doing that.

His ebony brows lifted. Hard disdain was etched on his patrician features as he observed, 'I wasn't. You're hardly glowing, are you?'

Determined not to show that his disparaging observation had shattered her confidence, she responded with laughing unconcern. 'Sorry you don't like my new cheekbones, but actually I'm more concerned with the fact I can actually look good in clothes now.' She glanced down and smoothed the skirt defiantly over her hips.

'You always looked good in clothes,' he retorted.

Lily searched his face expecting to find sarcasm. She found none.

'Though you looked a lot better without them.'

The silence that engulfed them seethed with things Lily wouldn't let herself analyse. The sound of her own tortured breathing was loud in her ears. Did the dark bands of colour along the slashing angle of Santiago's high cheekbones mean that he wasn't immune to the possibilities throbbing in the taut atmosphere…?

Did she want to find out?

'You're being so childish,' she stated defensively.

The harassed accusation ignited an astonished flare of anger in his deep-set eyes.

'Sorry,' she drawled. 'I forgot for a moment I was speaking to Santiago Morais. Obviously *you* couldn't be childish. You're brilliant and accomplished and incapable of putting a blessed foot wrong. Doesn't it ever get tiresome being so damned perfect?' He had been perfect in bed. The maverick thought sliced right through her anger and left her feeling uncomfortably defenceless.

'What the hell are you talking about?'

'Forget it. It's nothing you'd understand.' The problem, she reflected wearily, was that Santiago was one of those rare individuals who had never known failure. Had he ever failed at anything he decided to do? Lily studied his lean, autocratic features and doubted it. Failure simply wasn't in his vocabulary.

He folded the newspaper and put it on the table.

'I understand when someone is giving me the runaround.'

'I'm not trying to…' She gave a shrug. 'What's the point?' The spark might still be there between them, but it didn't matter what she said. There was no realistic possibility of them ever rekindling their affair.

Too much had happened.

He angled a disturbingly penetrative glance at her averted profile. 'Was that a question?'

Her eyes lifted and she squared her slumped shoulders. 'Don't worry. I'll make an excuse the first chance I get and leave.'

'You'll lie, you mean. Now why doesn't that surprise me?'

'Look, do you think I like this any better than you?' she demanded, dragging an exasperated hand over her forehead. She wasn't sure how much of this she could take. 'At least you knew what you were walking into. Can't we just make the best of what is an awkward situation?'

Santiago's jaw tightened a notch. '*Make the best of it…*' he repeated slowly. 'How very stoical and British of you.' His nostrils flared as he raked her with an openly contemptuous glance.

'I am British.'

A muscle clenched in his jaw. 'I, however, am not.'

Unnecessary information, she thought as he rose in one fluid motion to his feet.

'I am not stoical; I am Spanish.'

Despite the awfulness of the situation, or maybe because of it, the comment wrenched a laugh from her dry, aching throat. The heritage Santiago so proudly claimed had never been more apparent than at that moment.

'I was just thinking that it shows. You make being Spanish sound like a threat.'

'Do I…?' His shoulders lifted in a shrug, but he didn't deny the husky accusation. 'I am simply stating a fact. It is what I am.' His penetrative eyes continued to scan her face until she wanted to scream or run away…preferably both!

'Did you sleep well?'

At the innocuous enquiry some of the tension slid from

her body. 'Brilliantly,' she said, knowing the smudges of violet under her eyes, the ones she hadn't been able to totally disguise with make-up, gave lie to the claim.

'Then it must have been someone else I heard pacing the floor all night.'

'I don't pace.'

'*Really?* In case you forgot, your room is very near to mine, and one thing about these old houses is that the floor-boards creak.'

To hide the mortified colour that sprang to her cheeks Lily bent down and adjusted the strap of her sandal. 'I think we've already established I look like hell,' she grunted resentfully. 'I'm so sorry if I kept you awake.' She extended her bandaged hand. 'My hand was hurting.'

Something flickered behind his mesmeric eyes. 'It wouldn't be the first time you kept me awake,' he admitted throatily. 'Do you want me to look at it, change the bandage…?'

She shook her head, lowering her gaze protectively as the sexy rasp in his voice sent a debilitating shock through her body. Considering the stream of erotic images playing in her head, she managed to keep her voice remarkably expressionless as she added, 'It wasn't just that. Actually my bed is extremely uncomfortable and the pillows have rocks in.'

The extravagant fringe of lashes lifted, revealing the febrile glitter of his spectacular eyes. 'Mine isn't.'

The thud, thud of her treacherous heart made it hard for her to hear her own breathy response. 'Are you offering to swop? How very gentlemanly of you,' she quipped nervously.

'I was thinking more along the lines of…*sharing*?'

Her undiscriminating stomach muscles went into violent,

quivering spasm. 'I'll avoid the obvious been there and done that and simply say that sarcasm is hardly helpful.'

Presumably he *was* being sarcastic…the alternative made her heart beat faster. From under the fringe of her lashes, she scanned his face. It revealed nothing other than his perfect bone structure.

'Helpful to what?'

My blood pressure, she thought, staring at him help-lessly.

'And how do you know that wasn't a serious offer? I understand that you're a free agent these days.'

Lily stiffened, her expression growing wary. 'I'm di-vorced, but how—?'

With a voice like a scalpel he cut across her. 'Although being married never cramped your style, did it?'

She lifted her hands palm-up towards him in an uncon-scious gesture of submission. 'What am I supposed to say to that?'

Features set, he pressed a finger to the spot on his temple where he could feel a pulse throbbing. 'Being single doesn't suit you,' he rasped.

'Well, I'm enjoying it,' she lied immediately.

His critical dark eyes moved up and down her slim body. 'You look like you haven't had a decent meal in weeks, and don't give me that rubbish about a new image. For starters I think you'll discover the old image had more *pull-ing* power and, besides, your friend implied that you'd had problems.'

Expression blank, she shrugged.

With a muttered curse in his own tongue he turned and walked across the room. 'I suppose it was a man…?'

She looked at his broad back and gave a bitter little smile he couldn't see. 'I suppose you could say that,' she agreed drily. 'I'm surprised Rachel didn't fill in the details when you were discussing my private business.' The next time she got Rachel alone she was going to warn her not to say a word about the baby to Santiago unless she wanted her designer shoes trashed. 'Was it Rachel who told you about my divorce?'

'Dan. He said your husband dumped you? Not a secret, is it?'

'No, it's not a secret.' She looked at him and gave an exasperated sigh. 'Do you *have* to be so antagonistic?'

'You want to behave like we're old friends? Fine.' His mobile lips sketched a smile. 'Let's catch up…I know about the divorce, and I understand you're having a breakdown because of some man. Anything else of interest been happening?'

I was having your baby and I lost it…does that constitute interesting? Breathing hard, she bit back the retort that hovered unspoken on her tongue. She pressed a hand to her heaving chest until she trusted herself to speak.

'You're a callous bastard,' she announced conversationally. 'And I hate to disappoint you, but I'm not having a breakdown…although after this weekend who knows?' She released a laugh that even to her own ears sounded worryingly wild.

'And there's no need for you to tell me what you've been doing. It's been pretty well documented.' The gossip columns had been full of his latest romance.

'I'm flattered you take an interest.'

'I don't! *Nothing* you do is of any interest to me,' she proclaimed angrily.

One dark brow angled. '*Really?* Me, I have to admit to a certain curiosity. Your husband did leave you. Presumably one infidelity too many?'

She took a deep breath and forced her hands to unclench. '*One* was too many,' she hissed.

'Are you trying to tell me that I was the only one?' His mocking laugh grated against her raw nerve endings. 'I feel so special,' he confided nastily.

'I'm leaving. I must be mad to have stuck it out this long.'

'Leave…?'

Lily, already halfway to the door, stopped and half turned.

'Secure in the knowledge your concerned friend would run after you…'

'You didn't tell her about us, did you?' She sucked in a horrified breath.

'Was I meant to, *querida*?' Eyes narrowed to icy slits, Santiago slowly shook his dark head. 'How little you know me.'

'I wish I didn't know you at all!' she yelled back. After declaring childishly, 'I wish I'd never met you,' she ran from the room.

But did she? Did she *really* wish she had never met him? If she had a magic wand would she wipe out that short period of her life as if it had never been? Even after all the anguish and grief of the last year, would she deprive herself of the intense experience of falling in love?

CHAPTER NINE

'LILY, what do you think you're doing?'

Lily dropped the pile of wood she was carrying and turned around guiltily. 'Now look what you've made me do,' she grumbled, wiping a grubby hand across her face and leaving a dusty smudge along her cheek.

Rachel planted her hands on her slim hips. 'Put that down immediately! I can't leave you alone for a minute.'

'The doctor said light exercise is good for me. Besides, I like it.' The good thing about hard manual labour was, you got too tired to think—at least that was the theory. After the logs Lily planned to mow the lawn.

'I rather think the doctor had a gentle stroll in mind.'

'Then why didn't he say so?'

'I suppose he thought that he was talking to a rational human being,' Rachel retorted tartly before she turned to the tall man standing in the doorway. Her expression was accusing. 'Don't just stand there, pick it up!' She turned back to Lily. 'Anyone would think you *wanted* to hurt yourself?'

Lily didn't hear the exasperated comment. Her eyes were fixed on the tall, silent figure who had not responded yet to Rachel's terse command. How long had he been standing there and what, if anything, had he heard?

Their eyes connected, and it hit her like a sledgehammer—a massive surge of sheer longing. She didn't want to stop looking at his dark, sinfully beautiful, fallen-angel face, but she did.

The sun was hot, the night was dark, those were givens.

So was the fact that she would always be susceptible to Santiago's dark, dramatic looks. She might have to live with this mortifying fact, but she didn't have to put herself in a situation where she had to fight her own blind instincts.

In fact to do so would be criminally insane!

She squared her shoulders. 'Don't fuss, Rachel.' Her tone made Rachel's brows lift. 'Sorry, I didn't mean to snap, but I've had a toothache since last night,' Lily quickly improvised to explain her short temper.

'You have perfect teeth,' Rachel, who had spent a small fortune on cosmetic work to achieve a similar result, protested.

'Apparently not.'

Rachel scanned her face. 'You do look a bit off. How could you be so stupid?' she reproached. She laid a hand on her friend's arm. 'Come and sit down.'

'For heaven's sake, they're not heavy, and I'm not an invalid. It's been six months now.' The moment the words left her lips she knew they were a mistake.

Santiago, who so far had been silent, asked the one question he wasn't meant to. 'Six months since what?'

'Since nothing.'

'Since she lost the baby.'

The two contradictory statements emerged in unison.

Lily found herself looking directly into a dark pair of heavily fringed eyes, even though that was the one place she was trying hard not to look. So hard that beads of sweat had broken out along her upper lip. *Stay calm, Lily. He just looks as though he can read your mind. It's an illusion.*

Isn't it…?

There was a short, static silence before he said in a voice that was not so smooth and assured as normal, '*Baby…?*' His eyes dropped to her belly. 'You were pregnant.'

Lily was horrified to feel her eyes fill with weak tears.

Hand across her wet face, she turned; by the time she reached the stairs she was running. She didn't stop until she was in the small attic bedroom.

Rachel winced as the sound of the door slamming above made the cups on the dresser rattle. She felt obliged to offer an explanation for her friend's peculiar behaviour to this tall, urbane Spaniard.

'It's still a bit raw. She doesn't like to talk about it.' Her voice dropped to a soft, confidential whisper as she added, 'She was six months gone when they discovered there was no heartbeat.'

'The child died?' In contrast to the slow way he spoke his brain was making some rapid calculations. A man didn't need a calculator to figure the obvious maths. She had lost the child at six months, six months ago...the child could have been his.

Rachel, oblivious to the fact she was talking to a man who was anything other than mildly curious in the details, elaborated. 'To make things even worse she had to go through labour and deliver him knowing that...'

She sighed and shook her head as she watched Santiago, who had begun to mechanically stack the scattered logs into the basket by the door.

'It makes your heart break just to think about it,' she said half to herself. 'And then as if that wasn't enough something went wrong after the birth and they had to rush her to Theatre.'

There was a full thirty seconds' silence before Santiago straightened up. 'She had surgery?' He casually flicked a piece of cotton off his trousers.

Rachel wondered at his odd tone, but as his head was turned away from her as he examined his trousers for another invisible speck she couldn't read his expression. Though if last night was anything to go by that appeared the norm with Dan's Spanish mate. He was a stud, certainly, and she had seen flashes of humour, but she had been able to honestly soothe Dan the previous evening when she'd told him his distant Spanish cousin was much too intense and brooding for her taste.

'It was touch and go, apparently.'

His head came up and the expression on his rigid features startled Rachel. 'So that is why she has lost so much weight...' He turned to an astounded Rachel, his attitude harshly condemnatory. 'What were her family and friends doing while she wore herself to nothing?'

Driven on the defensive, Rachel responded apologetically to the abrupt demand. 'Well, she hasn't got any family since her gran died last year, and I and others have tried to help, but Lily is very proud...'

Santiago's nostrils flared. 'She is very stubborn.'

Rachel couldn't help but nod in agreement with this bitter observation. 'Tell me about it. I just wish I'd been in the country at the time.'

She might have paused to wonder how he suddenly seemed to know a lot about Lily, if he hadn't closed his eyes and exclaimed, in a low explosive undertone, *'Madre di Dios!'* The words emerged from between clenched teeth. 'She was all alone...?'

Carrying his child had almost killed her, and where had he been while she lay fighting for her life? It could have been any number of glitzy venues, all as instantly forgettable as each other. For a short time he had actually convinced himself that he had enjoyed the whirl of empty activity.

'Are you all right?' Rachel's concerned enquiry received no response. In fact her fellow house-guest gave no sign of having even heard her, as without saying another word he turned stiffly and strode out of the door, down the garden path and out into the lane.

'Now what was *that* about?' Rachel speculated, brushing a stray hair from her face as Santiago vanished from view down the leafy lane.

Spanish men were very unpredictable, she reflected, comparing this man's volatile behaviour with Dan's more predictable conduct. Of course Dan didn't have those eyes or that smile, she conceded, but you couldn't have everything.

She was beginning to suspect that hearing the details of Lily's ordeal had recalled some personal tragedy for Dan's friend. Hoping this wasn't the case, she went to see if Dan could shed some light on the situation.

Dan turned out to be in the car listening to the cricket score. She got in beside him and started recounting the incident; midway through she stopped, an arrested expression on her face.

'He said she'd lost weight. How did he know she'd lost weight?'

Dan looked puzzled, but not for the same reason as his girlfriend. 'Lost weight? She's fat.'

Rachel elbowed him in the ribs. 'She is not fat. It's the clothes she wears, silly. He must know her.'

Dan looked sceptical. 'If he knew her he'd have said so.'

'I suppose so,' Rachel conceded. 'Unless…'

'Unless what?'

'Dan, I think that he's Lily's Spanish waiter!'

Dan decided his beloved had lost her mind.

Unaware of the speculation going on, upstairs in her room Lily lay on the bed, her crooked arm lying across her tightly shut eyes. *I ran away.* She turned over and groaned. If she'd thought about it all day she couldn't have come up with a better way to arouse his suspicions.

Actually, she didn't know why she was so bothered. What did it matter if he found out? She tried to analyse her reluctance to share the truth with him. She'd had the perfect opportunity to explain when he'd brought up the subject of her appearance the day before.

She played out the scene in her head.

I would say—*I was pregnant, there were complications and I lost the baby.*

And he would think about it and ask—*Was it mine?*
Yes.

He would be shocked, of course; what man wouldn't? But as it sank in and he realised that there was no unwanted child to trouble his conscience, wouldn't he be secretly re-lieved for the narrow escape?

I don't want to see that relief!

She had lost a child that meant everything to her. She didn't expect Santiago to share her grief, but she didn't want to see the father of her child pay lip service when all the time he was thinking what a narrow escape he'd had.

Emotionally drained, she must have dozed because the next thing she knew someone was banging on her door. She lay there for a moment staring at the ceiling, wondering why she had a knot of tension in the pit of her stomach.

Then she remembered.

'Oh, God!' she groaned, pulling a pillow over her head. There was another urgent knock and the door-handle rat-tled. Lily tossed the pillow on the floor and sat up and rubbed her eyes. 'I'm asleep, Rachel. Go away.' One thing she definitely didn't feel like just now was an interrogation Rachel-style.

The door opened. 'It is not Rachel.'

Not unless Rachel had grown into a lean, muscle-packed,

The Harlequin Reader Service® — Here's how it works:

Accepting your 2 free books and 2 free mystery gifts places you under no obligation to buy anything. You may keep the books and gifts and return the shipping statement marked "cancel." If you do not cancel, about a month later we'll send you 6 additional books and bill you just $3.80 each in the U.S., or $4.47 each in Canada, plus 25¢ shipping & handling per book and applicable taxes if any.* That's the complete price and — compared to cover prices of $4.50 each in the U.S. and $5.25 each in Canada — it's quite a bargain! You may cancel at any time, but if you choose to continue, every month we'll send you 6 more books, which you may either purchase at the discount price or return to us and cancel your subscription.

*Terms and prices subject to change without notice. Sales tax applicable in N.Y. Canadian residents will be charged applicable provincial taxes and GST. All orders subject to approval. Credit or debit balances in a customer's account(s) may be offset by any other outstanding balance owed by or to the customer. Please allow 4 to 6 weeks for delivery.

If offer card is missing write to: Harlequin Reader Service, 3010 Walden Ave., P.O. Box 1867, Buffalo NY 14240-1867

NO POSTAGE
NECESSARY
IF MAILED
IN THE
UNITED STATES

BUSINESS REPLY MAIL

FIRST-CLASS MAIL   PERMIT NO. 717-003   BUFFALO, NY

POSTAGE WILL BE PAID BY ADDRESSEE

HARLEQUIN READER SERVICE
3010 WALDEN AVE
PO BOX 1867
BUFFALO NY 14240-9952

GET FREE BOOKS and FREE GIFTS WHEN YOU PLAY THE...

Lucky 7

SLOT MACHINE GAME!

Just scratch off the silver box with a coin. Then check below to see the gifts you get!

YES!
I have scratched off the silver box. Please send me the 2 free Harlequin Presents® books and 2 free gifts for which I qualify. I understand I am under no obligation to purchase any books, as explained on the back of this card.

306 HDL EF37   **106 HDL EF4Y**

FIRST NAME   LAST NAME

ADDRESS

APT.#   CITY

STATE/PROV.   ZIP/POSTAL CODE

7 7 7	**Worth TWO FREE BOOKS plus 2 BONUS Mystery Gifts!**
🍒🍒🍒	**Worth TWO FREE BOOKS!**
♣♣♣	**Worth ONE FREE BOOK!**
🔔🔔🍒	**TRY AGAIN!**

www.eHarlequin.com

(H-P-12/06)

Offer limited to one per household and not valid to current Harlequin Presents® subscribers.

six-foot-five male who oozed earthy sexuality from every delicious pore. After staring at the tall, dark figure who filled the doorway for a horror-stricken, open-mouthed moment, she recovered from her paralysis.

With as much dignity as the situation allowed she closed her mouth, swung her legs to the floor and tightened the knot of her pony-tail in a determined fashion.

'I can see that.' She eyed the intruder in a wary, unfriendly fashion and willed her racing heart to slow. 'Is dinner ready?' Even mentioning food made her stomach churn nauseously.

The furrow between his brows deepened as he looked at her as though she had lost her mind. 'I've not the faintest idea if dinner is ready.'

'Pity, I'm feeling quite peckish,' claimed Lily brightly. 'Then why…?' He didn't respond to her prompt, just carried on looking at her with a bone-stripping intensity that negated all her attempts to keep things light and normal.

Normal! Santiago Morais in your bedroom, normal? You should be so lucky, mocked the ironic voice in her head.

'What can I do for you, Santiago?' There had been a time when she would have meant that quite literally; she would have done anything for him.

'You can tell me if you were carrying my child.'

Lily gave up trying to be composed as with a sharp gasp she leapt to her feet and reached out as if to physically haul him into the room. 'For goodness' sake!' she cried. 'Lower your voice, and shut that door!'

Santiago did neither. 'I am waiting.'

She released a long, frustrated sigh through her clenched teeth. 'Closing the door was a suggestion, not an order, if that makes it easier for your macho pride. Now, please…please close the door before someone hears you,' she begged.

Santiago did as she requested, which was a mixed blessing as being inside the small room in his presence was almost unbearable. Even in the midst of her blind panic she felt dangerous swirls of excitement as their eyes touched. *Eyes to lose yourself in…*

'Now will you give me an answer?'

'Are they downstairs?' she asked in a hushed undertone.

He gave one of his maddening shrugs. The action made her belatedly aware that handfuls of his pale blue shirt were clamped between her clenched fingers.

'Sorry,' she mumbled, ineffectually patting the creased fabric. The fact she carried on patting just a bit too long might have had something to do with the hard, muscular contours of his perfectly developed upper arms.

All right, there was no *might* about it. Touching Santiago had always been addictive. In fact she hadn't been able to keep her hands off him, and he had always been more than willing to indulge her obsession, but not so now. He was looking down at her with an expression of impatient disdain etched on his hard features.

She mumbled a mortified, 'Sorry,' for the second time. 'I was afraid they might have heard you,' she explained, tucking her hands safely behind her back. Her thoughts, the ones that involved her hands gliding over satiny golden and perfectly formed hard muscles, were less easily disposed of.

'Your friends knowing we have been lovers bothers you?'

Lovers. He sounded so indifferent when he said it, as though he were discussing the weather, but hearing their relationship described this way in his deep accented voice sent an illicit shiver through her hopelessly receptive body.

'Too right it bothers me,' she grunted, lifting a hand to her tangled hair as she watched him lean against the wall.

Unless his fitness levels had decreased dramatically the shallow flight of stairs that led to her room could not account for the rapid rise and fall of his chest.

'The truth bothers you.'

'I don't like to advertise my mistakes,' she stressed in response to his sarcastic interjection. 'And you were the one who acted as though we had never met when I arrived.' She heard the note of dissatisfaction in her voice and almost groaned out loud.

Santiago's lips formed an ironic smile as he recalled the moment he saw her standing there. Every time he thought about those seconds before his self-control and pride had kicked in, the moment when fierce delight had permeated every cell of his body, he experienced a wave of self-disgust.

'I was just following your lead.'

This outrageously false claim drew a snort of derision from her dry throat. 'Well, that would be a first.'

He gave a dangerous grin that didn't reach the hardness in his eyes. 'Meaning what, exactly?'

Quiet mad. Santiago did quiet mad well, but then Santiago did *everything* well! The thought inevitably took her in the direction of the bedroom. She closed that mental door and in a burst of reckless frustration she told him exactly what she meant.

'Meaning that you never follow *anyone's* lead, certainly not mine. You are autocratic, overbearing and it never even occurs to you that people won't do exactly what you want them to. You see something you want and take it regardless of the consequences. I can see how this dark, brooding Spanish-lover thing has worked for you over the years, but a word to the wise…if you want a long-term relationship, you'd better start giving a little more and taking a little less!' she finished on a breathless, bitter quiver.

Even though she felt good at that moment, she was pretty sure she'd regret her cathartic diatribe—if she could remember exactly what she'd said, that was. It was already a bit of a worrying blur.

His eyes were hot as if lit from within as he responded in a husky voice that vibrated through Lily all the way to her toes.

'I was under the impression that I took nothing you were not anxious to give to me.'

And I gave and gave... Lily veered her thoughts firmly in the opposite direction. Her chin was up, but she couldn't prevent the flush that ran up under her fair skin as their eyes met.

Her recent emotional outburst took its inevitable toll as, without warning, her knees folded under her. Fortunately the bed was there to break her fall...

'I wasn't looking for a husband,' she said bitterly. 'Just a bit of fun.'

'I was light relief?' The muscle in his lean cheek throbbed like a time bomb and she couldn't tear her fascinated eyes from it.

'What else?'

If Santiago had been angry before, he was furious now. Her heart climbed into her throat as she watched him struggle to contain his feelings of outrage.

'You already had a husband, didn't you, Lily? Though I wonder at your choice of...playmate. I'm amazed you were prepared to sleep with such an arrogant, selfish, abusing bastard.' Through his long dark lashes she could see the furious glitter of his jet eyes and they had a strangely mesmeric effect upon her.

'I didn't know you when I slept with you, and you're not selfish in bed.'

She heard his splintered gasp and froze suddenly because

instead of hostility the room seethed with an equally volatile, but infinitely more dangerous, emotion—the sexual charge hung heavy in the air between them.

'Neither are you,' he admitted thickly.

Through the open window she could hear bird song. The carefree sound provided a sharp contrast to the tense atmosphere in the room.

'Like I said before, it was a mistake. One I'm not terribly proud of.'

Something dark and dangerous flared in his eyes as his brooding features hardened. She watched as his clenched hands unbunched. Very slowly he exhaled silently and folded his arms across his chest. 'And did that ''mistake'' include getting pregnant?'

CHAPTER TEN

STRICKEN to silence, Lily just looked at Santiago.

'It is not a difficult question so why is it so hard for you to answer?'

Good question.

And one Lily had never anticipated having to answer. She hadn't thought she would ever see Santiago again. To lie was the simplest and most expedient solution. Yes, it was almost definitely the way to go, and she opened her mouth to do just that, but strangely the required words wouldn't come.

She walked across the room and straightened an already straight insipid print on the wall and twitched a curtain.

As the silence lengthened a spasm of impatience twisted Santiago's mobile mouth. Her dark curling lashes gave her very little protection when his interrogative gaze locked onto her flustered face. *'Well...?'* he rapped, obviously holding on to his temper with difficulty.

Her lips formed a mutinous line. 'Well what?'

She heard the audible snap as his white teeth came together in a frustrated grimace. 'I know how much you like playing games, Lily,' he said, levering himself off the wall and rotating his broad shoulders in a way that made her visualise the knots of tension in his tight muscles that he was trying to relieve.

She could recall smoothing away the tension, letting her fingers glide over his smooth, oiled skin.

His expression was set and bleak as he added softly, 'But, believe me, now is not the time.'

Neither was it the time to get distracted by a sexual fantasy, but she was doing it anyhow. She bit back the bubble of hysterical laughter that rose to her lips. 'I don't play games. And I'd like you to leave my room.' The latter was said with no real belief he would do so.

He didn't.

'And *I* want to know if you were carrying my child.'

Lily dragged her eyes clear of the frenetic nerve spasming beside his wide, sensual mouth—never a good idea to look at his mouth—and she stuck out her chin. Despite the body language inside she felt about as defiant as a limp lettuce leaf. She took a deep sustaining breath and angled an enquiring look up at his dark lean face.

'Why do you want to know?'

Santiago's jaw clenched; he looked at her in furious disbelief. '*Why?* Are you *serious*?'

The colour began to creep into her pale cheeks. 'It seems a reasonable question to me.'

'You know nothing about reason!' he contended loudly.

'Will you lower your voice?' Lily yelled back even louder.

'You know nothing about the truth! You...' With a visible effort he controlled himself and gritted, 'I warn you, Lily...'

'Warn me?' she parroted, breathing as hard as he was now. There had been times when she had needed him, when she had wanted him and he hadn't been there. No, he turned up now, just when she was about to put her life back together again...*typical*! She looked at his hands clenched white-knuckled at his sides. Clever hands that had moved with infinite variety over her tingling flesh... *Don't go there, Lily!*

The instruction came too late. A visceral shudder was

already passing through her body as heat ignited deep in her belly.

'What the hell right do you have to warn me about anything?' she demanded, shrilly desperate as she tried to ignore what was happening. 'We only slept together.' She dug deep and managed a more than passable 'so what?' shrug.

The effort produced a rash of cold sweat over her body. But maybe, she reasoned, if she annoyed him enough he might get sidetracked and forget his original objective. 'It's history, and not a very important piece of history at that.'

Strangely objective, she watched his nostrils flare and the strong, beautifully sculpted lines of his incredible face tighten until the golden skin pulled taut and glistening with a fine sheen of moisture across the angles of his jutting cheekbones. He looked the epitome of Southern Mediterranean fury as he loosed a flood of low, hoarse words in his native tongue.

He was awesome!

He really was the most incredible-looking man. *Excitement…?* It was with horror that Lily identified the illicit thrill that tingled along her raw nerve endings.

Even in the midst of his fury Santiago's hot eyes strayed to Lily's slim, ringless fingers that plucked fretfully at the neckline of her tight-fitting sweater. The deep vee gave a tantalising hint of the creamy swell of her soft breasts, whose fullness was emphasised by the extreme slenderness of the rest of her body. His already rock-hard body reacted violently to the feminine image.

'What's the point?' She smiled and recklessly ignored the hoarse growl of incredulity that issued from his throat. 'Think about it,' she advised. 'I mean, what difference does it make? There isn't a baby…*not now.*'

Santiago flinched at the bleak little addition, but his expression didn't soften. 'Was the child mine, Lily? I'm asking for a yes or no. How hard is that?'

Extremely hard, she knew that, it was the why she couldn't figure. Why couldn't she just say, Yes, I was having your baby, end of story?

'You know we used…we were c-careful.' Or at least *he* had been. It shamed Lily to be forced to admit that the desperate urgency Santiago had aroused within her had been matched by a negligence to consider the consequences that in retrospect horrified her.

He pointed out the obvious. 'Careful doesn't always work,' he said bluntly. 'The only sure form of contraception is celibacy.'

The comment made Lily wonder about all the women who had fallen for his fatal charm since they had parted. 'Not really your style, is it?'

His upper lip curled. 'And it's yours…?'

Lily flushed and desperation drove her to retort defensively, 'It was purely physical.'

His dark eyes signalled contempt as they swept across her flushed face. 'And here was I thinking it was a meeting of souls. Imagine my devastation.' His sarcastic drawl tautened as he added, 'I am asking you for the last time, were you carrying my child?'

'I don't respond well to ultimatums, Santiago.'

Her delaying tactics were beginning to have visible effect on his anger. 'And I don't respond well to being lied to, Lily.'

'I haven't lied to you.'

One dark brow arched sardonically at her protest. A tide of hot colour rose up to Lily's hairline. Her shoulders slumped, she gave a tiny nod of assent. 'I think the baby was yours.'

'*Think…?*'

Lily barely heard him, the feelings were rushing back, and for a moment she could feel the tiny body in her arms. The pain and loss, the feelings of total hopelessness, threatened to overwhelm her. She barely registered Santiago's hands on her shoulders forcing her to sit down. He then dropped down on his haunches so that his dark face was level with hers.

'Take some deep breaths,' he ordered.

The concern underlying the rough instruction made her look at him. Their faces were close, close enough for her to see the individual lines radiating from his deep-set eyes and the tiny silver pinpricks of light deep in the darkness of the irises. She inhaled a quivering breath that drew in the warm male scent of his body, evoking forbidden memories.

The memories caused the empty, aching feeling in the pit of her belly to intensify. She felt his fingers tighten against her collar-bone just before his hands fell away completely.

'Don't be nice to me,' she begged huskily. That, she reflected, shouldn't be too hard for him. Not that he hadn't had cause to be mean to her. She had let him think she'd been single when she'd still been married; that constituted just cause in most people's book.

She had *tried* to explain she hadn't set out to deceive him, that it had just happened, but he hadn't wanted to listen to her explanations. Then in her turn she had got angry.

'Come off it, Santiago. Are you trying to tell me that you've never lied to a woman to get her into bed…?' She deliberately goaded him with a light, scornful laugh when he confronted her with her deceit.

For a split second she thought he was going to throttle her. Then he too laughed, a harsh laugh that sent a chill down her spine. 'You didn't have to lie to get me into your bed, *querida*.' His contempt seemed aimed as much at himself as her.

Lily couldn't let this sort of blatant hypocrisy pass without comment. 'I thought you didn't sleep with married women.'

'*I don't!*' he gritted back. The explosive silence that followed his words lengthened until a full minute had passed before he added, 'For you I would have made an exception.'

'Because I'm irresistible?' she fired back with withering sarcasm.

Something hot that made her stomach flip moved behind those dark, impenetrable eyes. '*Yes.*'

She sucked in her breath and felt the heat travel through her body. '*Santiago…?*' Her husky voice was infused with entreaty that it later shamed her to recall as she reached out to him, emotionally and physically.

In hindsight she recognised that moment as one of those crossroads in life, the ones that you didn't know you stood at until later. If he had reached out and taken her hand, as she was sure he almost had, things might have turned out differently.

But he hadn't.

'I'll do my best not to be too nice,' he promised. Her expression vague and distracted, her big blue eyes meshed with his as the past collided with the present. With a soft cry she turned her head.

'No!' He caught her chin in his fingers. 'Don't turn away, Lily,' he said, angling her face back to his.

Lily felt as if her heart would break. 'I think your best will be more than sufficient,' she croaked back.

His lips formed a twisted smile. 'So now I am a brutal monster, am I?'

She shook her head. 'No,' she admitted huskily, 'but you have a very cruel tongue when you're angry.' And when he had discovered she had lied to him, when he had discovered that she had still been married, he had been *very* angry.

'*Madre mia*, but it's true.'

The angry admission surprised her.

'You have this strange ability to bring out the extremes in my personality. Be it anger...' his eyes dropped to the soft outline of her mouth '...or passion...' She gasped and drew back fractionally as his thumb brushed her lower lip.

A deep sigh vibrated through her body as her eyes half closed and her body swayed towards him as though drawn by an invisible thread.

Neither of them spoke while she stayed with her head resting against his chest. When she eventually raised her head she took a step away from him and absently swept the wispy strands of hair from her face with her forearm.

She took a deep, resolute sigh. 'Right, what do you want to know?' she asked, connecting with his sombre eyes.

'When did you...when did...?'

She had no problem understanding what he was trying to ask. 'I was in the sixth month,' she cut in quietly.

'Sixth month.' She watched the muscles in his brown throat move as he swallowed convulsively.

'Babies sometimes live when they are born at that stage? Is that not so?'

She nodded. 'But my baby was already dead,' she told him huskily, while in her head she relived that awful moment when the young woman doing the scan had given her a bright professional smile and excused herself. *I just need to go and get the doctor,* she had said.

The professional smile had not fooled Lily; she had known that something was wrong. The doctor, with his kind, tired eyes, had held her hand when he'd told her.

'You're sure…you're absolutely sure?'

'Yes, though naturally we will double-check. Can I contact your husband…partner…?'

She had shook her head. 'No, he isn't…he's not around any longer.'

'Is there someone you'd like me to contact?'

'No, I'll be fine, thank you.'

'*Our* baby.'

Still trapped in a nightmare of recollections Lily lifted her eyes to Santiago's face. She shook her head. 'Sorry…?'

'Our baby. The child you were carrying was *our* child, and apparently it did not occur to you to tell me?' His low voice was flat and devoid of expression; not so the blazing eyes that were fixed on her face.

'I suppose I had other things on my mind.' Lily, whose face moments earlier had been snow-white, was now suffused with angry colour. 'There was no conspiracy to keep you in the dark.'

'From where I'm sitting that's hard to believe.'

'Well, believe it or not, it's true. I was waiting for the right time.' Even to Lily this sounded lame.

'How hard was it to pick up the phone and tell me?'

'And you'd have believed me, I suppose?' she charged. 'Right, that was *very* likely.' Despite her defiant attitude, she was actually shaken by the depth of his reaction. 'I had to think about what I'd do if you wanted to go down the DNA court-case route.'

His darkly defined brows twitched into an interrogative line above his aquiline nose as he gave a baffled frown. '*Court case…?*'

'Isn't that how it works when a celebrity dad denies paternity?'

His lips twisted in distaste. 'I am not a celebrity.'

'You do things and people write about them. You have more money than any one person could spend in a lifetime. In fact,' she accused, 'I bet you don't even know how much money you have.'

He didn't deign to respond to this angry claim, but said in a taut, controlled voice, 'I do not court publicity, and I protect my private life.'

'You didn't protect it much when you took Susie Sebastian *almost* wearing *that* dress to the music awards...' she began darkly.

'Shall we leave aside for one moment the definition of celebrity? We are talking about you keeping me in the dark about my child.'

Lily wouldn't leave it alone. 'Newspapers don't pay you for stories about people unless they're celebrities.'

His brows lifted. 'Should I expect to see a kiss-and-tell story in the tabloids in the near future?'

Her lips formed a mirthless smile. 'Very funny.' *Maybe he's serious.* Her eyes flew to his face, and what she saw in them soothed her suspicions. At least he didn't think she was capable of that. 'My finances are not stretched that thin yet.' Actually, they probably were. She pushed the worrying state of her bank balance to one side for a moment and added provocatively, 'But who knows in the future...?'

'Why would you assume that I would have denied paternity?'

She tilted her head to look into his dark, hostile eyes and shrugged. 'Well, you must admit the idea of you embracing fatherhood under those circumstances is worth the odd laugh.'

'Do you see me laughing?'

CHAPTER ELEVEN

LILY accepted the invitation and studied Santiago's dark, lean face. She felt the first flicker of uncertainty.

'Your actions were based on the assumption that I wouldn't have wanted to take a full and active role in my child's life. I think that's a pretty big assumption to make, don't you...?'

'So what...are you saying you'd have proposed?'

'That would have been difficult, as you were already married, wouldn't it, Lily?' Lily was too startled to resist when without warning he took her left hand in his. She watched as he looked at her index finger and then, turning her hand over, looked at the palm.

She found it impossible to look away as he stroked the soft skin. The hand that wasn't captured curled into a tight fist as she tensed. She winced as the action caused the bandage to dig into her skin.

'You've taken off your rings.'

'I gave them to a charity shop.' She pulled her hand away. 'Gordon was furious. And,' she reflected absently, 'he was probably right. It was a grand gesture I can't afford.'

'If I had been there to make you take care of yourself our baby might have lived.' He exhaled a long, shuddering sigh and, head in his hands, sank down onto the bed beside her.

Lily froze and missed totally the strong element of self-condemnation in his voice. She heard only the accusation, the levelling of blame. Santiago had hit a raw nerve.

Despite the doctor's repeated assertions that what had happened would have happened no matter what she had done, Lily hadn't totally shaken off the guilt that had afflicted her after the miscarriage.

'You're saying it was my fault…?' Her voice cracked as she added with a harsh laugh, 'I suppose you think I'd have made a terrible mother.'

'At least you'd have had the opportunity to try.' He met her blank look of incomprehension with a twisted smile. 'I was never going to have the opportunity to even meet my son, let alone be his father. Years in the future I could have passed my own son in the street and not known him!' His accusing eyes swung back to her. 'You would have denied me my son.'

Her face suddenly crumpled. 'We were both denied our son.' Biting back the sobs that refused to be subdued, she pressed her hands to her face and turned her back on him.

For a moment Santiago watched the grief-stricken figure before he reached across and pulled her roughly into his arms.

'I'm sorry. It must have been a terrible experience for you, but it's just I've learnt I had a child and lost him all in an hour.'

Lily lifted her tear-stained face from his chest. 'I'd say time makes it better, but I'm not sure it would be true.'

Santiago took her pony-tail in his hand and wrapped the gleaming strands around his fingers. 'You've had a hell of a time, haven't you? I don't want you to take this the wrong way, but I need to know something.'

'Then you'd better ask.'

'Were you going to pass the baby off as your husband's?'

Lily stiffened. Shaking with anger, she lifted her shimmering eyes to his. 'You are the most hateful man I know!'

Her voice ached with feeling as she leapt from the bed and backed away.

'I don't know why you look so outraged...'

The man was just unbelievable! 'You just accused me of passing off another man's child as my husband's. How do you expect me to look?'

'You didn't answer the question.'

'And I'm not going to.'

'You would hardly be the first woman to do so and under the circumstances it was a perfectly legitimate question.'

'What circumstances?'

'As you have pointed out, I know to my cost that lying is second nature to you...and even if you hadn't slept with him during the relevant period you could have been vague about the dates.'

Not when the relevant period had been nearly a year. 'For your information, when Gordon left me I didn't even know I was pregnant.'

'And when you did your first thought was to tell the father.'

His ironic tone made her delicate jaw tighten. 'It's really easy for you to act all hurt and offended now...now there isn't a baby.' She blinked as her eyes filled with the sting of hot tears.

'Actually things worked out pretty well for you, didn't they?' she accused in a voice that shook with emotion. 'Now there is no baby.'

'You think this makes me happy!' he yelled furiously.

'And, anyhow, I couldn't have passed the baby off as Gordon's. We hadn't even...' She stopped and flushed to the roots of her hair. 'Well, anyway,' she ended lamely, 'I didn't.'

'You hadn't even what?' His eyebrows lifted. 'Had sex...?'

Lily struggled to maintain a semblance of calm, though inside she was shaking with anger. 'I have no intention of discussing my private life with you.'

He directed a speculative look at her pale face. 'Is that why you slept with me? You wanted a child? And your husband wasn't willing, or able?'

'You really think that I'm that manipulative?'

His eyes slid from hers as he slowly shook his head as the anger left his body. 'No.' The sweep of his long lashes lifted from his cheekbones. 'You do realise when it must have happened, don't you? It must have been the first time.'

Her eyes slid from his. 'Probably,' she admitted, trying not to think about warm air caressing her naked skin.

It hadn't even crossed her mind that she would ever be uninhibited enough to make love out of doors. Not that the place had been exactly public. The mountain restaurant had been just as remote as Santiago had suggested. Lily hadn't seen a single other car on the journey there and when Santiago had drawn the car onto a grassy verge on the way back they still hadn't encountered another living soul.

'Why are we stopping?'

'Not for the reason you think.'

'How do you know what I think?' she countered crossly.

'It's written all over your beautiful face. Come on,' he urged, sliding out of the driving seat. 'I want you to see something.'

He took her by the hand and led her through a copse of tall cedar trees. As they cleared the trees she gasped.

'It's incredible, isn't it?' he said, gazing out at the view stretched out before them. 'You can see for miles.'

'Yes, incredible.'

Santiago turned his head and caught her looking at him, not the view. She saw the surprise in his eyes, followed by the heat. Lily could have pretended he was wrong, that she wasn't looking at him and thinking he was more gorgeous than any view, but she didn't. She just carried on looking at him.

'Are we trespassing?'

'No, I own it,' he said huskily.

'You bought it?' She looked at his mouth and wanted very badly to kiss him.

'It's a special place and you are a special person, Lily.'

Lily could remember the emotional thickness in her throat making her unable to speak when he took her face between his hands. 'Maybe we should go back,' he said, releasing her almost immediately.

She shook her head and, lower lip caught between her teeth, looked up at him through her eyelashes. 'Couldn't we stay just a little longer?' She watched his eyes darken and felt quite dizzy with power.

His eyes slid down her body, his stillness had an explosive quality. 'That's not a good idea,' he said huskily.

Her chin lifted. 'I don't want to be good.'

She heard him inhale sharply and, smiling, pushed her hands under his shirt. She laid them flat against his warm, tight belly and felt the sharp contraction of his muscles. His skin was warm and satiny textured; low in her pelvis things tightened and shifted. She closed her eyes and, head thrown back a little, sighed with unconcealed pleasure as she began to stroke him, light, teasing movements that drew a faint groan from his throat.

'You have absolutely no idea how much I wanted to touch you,' she revealed, watching him breathe in and out fast. To want someone this much was scary and wildly exciting at the same time. 'All the while we were talking I wanted to touch you.' She saw the beads of sweat break out across his upper lip.

'I'm getting the idea,' he said, sounding slightly breathless.

Lily thought about her bare skin touching his and, shivering, she slid her fingers lower down his belly. With a muttered imprecation he pulled back and caught both her wrists to prevent her fingertip exploration getting any more intimate.

He doesn't want me!

Before the humiliation could totally crush her, Lily connected with his eyes and felt a surge of relief. Those were not the eyes of a man who was about to reject her. They were the eyes of a man who was clinging to the shreds of his self-control. *One push,* she thought, watching his jaw clench.

'You don't know what you're doing,' he accused.

She smiled and leaned forward until her lips were about a centimetre away from his mouth. 'I know exactly what I'm doing,' she said against his lips.

He sucked in a deep breath, then with a soft curse grabbed her face between his hands. The driven ferocity in his kiss made her dissolve. With a soft cry of relief she kissed him back with everything she had.

He carried on kissing her until her knees gave way instead of supporting her. Santiago slid down to the floor with her, pulling her body on top of him.

For a second she didn't move, just lay there wondering what was going to happen next. Then he said, *'Kiss me. I want you to kiss me.'*

It was a good sign, she decided as she pressed her mouth to his, that they seemed to both want the same things. Santiago did several things she hadn't even known she had wanted until he did them!

A shudder ran through Lily's body as, suddenly drawn

back to the present, she banished the steamy images of their two naked bodies intimately entwined from her head.

She swallowed and looked at Santiago. His skin was covered in a light sheen of sweat, and the feverish brilliance in his painfully expressive eyes told her that she hadn't been the only one revisiting that memory.

Sharing memories was almost like foreplay. The shocking idea sent a thrill of heat through her body.

Santiago let his glance move from hers to the bed, then slowly back to her flushed face.

She knew she should make it clear that this wasn't going to happen. She didn't; neither of them spoke. Words weren't needed.

Lily was conscious only of his dark, mesmeric eyes, and the need that burned inside her as they kissed, not gently, but with a raw, bruising urgency. Then when they broke apart he took her hand and led her to the bed.

Lily let him pull her down beside him and they lay side by side, not touching, just breathing hard.

Lily tried to understand how this could be so mindblowingly erotic when he was not even touching her. When he did she sucked in a deep, shocked breath and felt everything inside tighten.

'The thing I remember is how, whenever I touched you, you were always hot.' The hand that was on her hip slid a little lower as he added thickly, 'And ready for me.'

Lily licked her lips, so aroused she could barely breathe. When his hand moved under her skirt she stuck her fist in her mouth to stop herself yelling out. He touched the lacy edge of her knickers and she could no longer stop herself moaning.

'That's right, let go,' he rasped, watching her face as he parted her legs and slid his fingers into the soft, warm heat between.

'Oh, my God!' she moaned, pushing against his hand and squirming. 'I want…'

'You want me.'

'I want you,' she sobbed as he lifted her skirt around her hips. *'Right now,'* she added from between clenched teeth.

She reached for him, fumbling with the clasp of his belt. He took her shaking hands and pinioned them above her head with one hand, while with the other he completed the job she hadn't been able to. He left her for a moment, but only to rip off his shirt and kick aside his jeans.

Lily held onto the bars of the headboard, her body arching as he slid into her. He felt so incredible that she wanted to cry. She closed her eyes and felt his breath come heavy and hot against her neck as he began to move. She moved with him, gasping, feeling the familiar pressure slowly building inside her to a dark rhythm she could feel roaring in her blood.

Then without warning the wave she was riding broke and pleasure, wave after wave of nerve-tingling pleasure, exploded through her body.

CHAPTER TWELVE

IT WAS the sort of thing you wondered about. What would you do if you put your foot on the brake and nothing happened?

Lily had never actually expected to find out.

The situation was complicated by the bend she was fast approaching and the double-decker bus coming in the opposite direction.

Was this the moment her life was meant to flash before her eyes? Lily's didn't; she was too busy trying to save her skin. She succeeded. A nifty bit of steering, some frantic use of the gears and a lot of luck landed her on the grass verge with the front end of her car wedged in a hedge.

The car door, partially against a branch, was difficult to open, but after a short, determined tussle she emerged scratched by the brambles but otherwise unharmed.

The bus driver was inclined to want to yell at her, she couldn't blame him, but when she explained that her brakes had failed he calmed down and even said a few nice things about her driving skills.

The horse and rider she had driven at a snail's pace past a few hundred yards back reached them and she began the explanations all over again.

'I thought I was going to hit her for sure,' the bus driver confessed, wiping his forehead with his sleeve. 'Have you ever seen a car after it's hit a double-decker head-on?' he asked. Nobody had. 'There's not much to see.'

Everyone laughed, except Lily, who was starting to experience what she assumed was a delayed reaction to the shock. She clenched her teeth and tried to stop them jarring against each other.

'What's the procedure? Do I call the police or a recovery service?' Lily asked, trying to stay focused and practical.

'My God, you were lucky!' one of the passengers who had left the bus remarked for the third time.

Lily, who was starting to realise just how lucky, nodded and felt sick. The adrenaline rush that had got her through the ordeal this far was definitely bottoming out and her knees were literally shaking. She was looking around for somewhere to sit down when a big, gleaming, low-slung car drew to a halt a couple of yards away.

The occupant took in the scene of near averted disaster and was heard to swear at length. Although it was hard to be positive on this point because he was talking a foreign language. The group of people around Lily fell silent when he vaulted athletically from the vehicle and stalked towards them, looking like a dark avenging angel in designer sunglasses.

Oh, no, he'd followed her!

Lily dabbed her dry lips nervously with the tip of her tongue as the tall figure approached. Pale but resolute, she waited to be the target of his blistering anger, as she usually was.

Santiago was angry. Possibly, he recognised, *more* angry than he had ever felt in his entire life, but then why should that surprise him? he reflected bitterly. This woman was capable of extracting the most extreme emotional response from him.

On this occasion he actually embraced the anger that seethed through his veins because it was infinitely preferable to what had gone before. He never wanted to feel the way he had when he had broached the hill and seen Lily's car slewed across the road and embedded in the hedge. He never wanted to relive those seconds when he had thought the worst, but he suspected he was doomed to in his nightmares for some time to come.

'Hello, Santiago.' She had never been so glad to see anyone in her life, which was totally irrational considering she had been driving away from the cottage to avoid seeing him when her brake had failed.

'Hello,' he echoed. The simple greeting made his eyes flash. *'Hello…?'* he repeated, dragging a hand through his dark hair as he scanned her face.

There was no visible damage to Lily other than torn clothes and a few scratches. The nightmare images of mangled bodies were still there, but they were receding as he realised she seemed to have escaped the impact apparently unscathed.

His big hands settled on her shoulders and in a husky voice he enquired, 'Are you hurt?'

Lily assumed that he was running his hands down her body to check her out for injury. Unfortunately her response to the light clinical examination was anything but clinical.

'What are you doing here?'

'What do you think I'm doing here? I woke up and you were gone.'

'Don't shout!' Lily begged, painfully aware of their interested audience. 'Didn't Rachel tell you I remembered an appointment I just had to keep?'

'Do not insult my intelligence; I am not your gullible friend. And, just for the record, after Rachel walked in and found me asleep and stark naked in your bed I doubt she's falling for the appointment story either.'

'She didn't!' Lily gasped in horror.

'She did and…' Santiago stopped and scanned her paper-white face. 'Sit down before you fall down.'

'I'm fine,' she croaked. Actually her ribs where the seat belt had cut in were beginning to ache. Later, she recognized, they would be painful.

Her claim seemed to inflame him further. 'And would you tell me if you weren't?' The band of dark colour etched along the ridge of his sharp cheekbones deepened as he drew in a deep, unsteady breath.

Deeply conscious of the thumbs that were now resting on the crest of her hip-bones—his fingers were curved possessively across her bottom—she tried to resist the almost overwhelming impulse to simply sink against him.

'You're acting as if I drove into the hedge just to irritate you.'

'It wouldn't surprise me if you had,' he contended grimly. 'How could you be so criminally careless?' he wanted to know, lifting a hand from her bottom, but only to roughly stroke the hair back from her cheek.

She tried to sound matter-of-fact as she explained what had happened. 'The brakes failed.' Her breathing quickened as she experienced the moment of panic a second time.

The colour seeped from his olive-toned skin as he sucked in a deep shuddering breath. If Lily hadn't closed her eyes in a futile attempt to blot out the images in her head she would have seen the strain that was evident in the taut lines of his lean face.

'Yes, I put my foot down and nothing happened, and there was a bus coming…so…'

His hand fell from her face. '*Failed…?*' His oddly flat voice cut across her.

'Yes, they failed. I'm trying to explain.'

'Explain! What is there to explain?' The muscles in his throat worked as he swallowed. '*Madre mia*, what is wrong with you? You drive around dangerous roads in a car that is clearly fit only for the scrap heap. Heaven knows how you escaped serious injury.'

'Just because it didn't cost a fortune, and doesn't go at a hundred miles an hour, doesn't mean it's not roadworthy. For your information it passed its MOT last month.'

'Whoever passed it should be flogged.'

This brutal conclusion made Lily blink. 'It was just an accident.'

Her weak protest triggered another long stream of Spanish curses. 'It was an accident. It wasn't my fault. No, it's never *your* fault, is it? Nothing is your fault. You blithely go through life wrecking lives left, right and centre and it's *never* your fault.'

Lily lifted a hand to her brow in a fluttery motion. The unsteady gesture made her look intensely vulnerable, which irrationally made Santiago more livid than ever.

The red dots dancing before her eyes had begun to thicken to a mist. Through it she could see his face as a dark blur. 'Whose life have I wrecked?'

'Yours…mine…' she heard him say thickly just before she slithered gracefully to the ground.

Lily was only out for a couple of minutes. When she came to she found she was lying on the grass verge with something warm and heavy draped over her. Someone was holding her wrist between their fingers.

'Her pulse is strong.'

The fingers left her wrist.

The warm and heavy thing smelt of Santiago. His jacket? She half opened her eyes and discovered she was right. The two men continued to talk above her.

'Like I said, she just fainted, mate. I wouldn't worry.'

'Yes, I am fine,' said Lily.

'I told you so,' said the bus driver as Santiago squatted down beside her prone figure.

'How do you feel?' he asked, scanning her face.

'I'm fine,' she repeated and tried to sit up. Santiago's hand on her chest pinned her gently but firmly to the ground.

'You will not move until the ambulance arrives.'

She decided not to fight him on this, mostly because when she did move her head swam unpleasantly. 'Fine, have it your way.'

He sketched a grim smile. 'I intend to.'

So nothing new there. 'So you expect me to lie here…?'

'Yes.'

She eased herself up on one elbow and this time met with no resistance. 'How about if I move six inches to the left…?'

Santiago settled back onto his heels. 'Why?'

'I'm lying on a dirty great rock; it's sticking in my back. I'll be black and blue tomorrow.'

'You'll be alive tomorrow,' Santiago retorted grimly as she shuffled away from the offending item.

He lifted his head and frowned into the distance. 'Where is that damned ambulance…?'

When he turned back to her, still frowning, Lily noticed for the first time the signs of extreme tension in his face. The most noticeable clue was the greyish tinge of his normally vibrant skin tone.

'I don't need an ambulance. Do I look like I need an ambulance?' she asked, pushing aside his jacket. 'Talk about an overreaction,' she grumbled tetchily. 'And I thought you were the sort of man who would be useful in a crisis.'

'I have no interest in what *you* think you need. Or what you think of me.' This demonstration of his high-handed attitude brought an angry frown to her face. 'And I don't think you have the faintest idea what is good for you,' he continued patronisingly.

'You could be right, but I do know what is bad for me.' She glared pointedly at his face.

He rolled his eyes. 'And yet here we are together again.'

'That's not any of my doing,' she retorted. 'You shouldn't have followed me.'

'What did you expect me to do? You left before I woke up.'

She swallowed. 'I thought you'd be relieved. Goodbyes are always awkward.'

'I had no intention of saying goodbye.'

To her intense frustration the sound of an ambulance siren meant she didn't get to hear what he had intended to say.

When the ambulance reached the local hospital Santiago was already standing outside the casualty department. How someone who could beat an ambulance to the hospital had the cheek to criticise her driving beat her; clearly he was allowed to risk his life.

A couple of hours later a doctor armed with X-ray results and her medical notes gave her a clean bill of health. 'I'm afraid you're going to be pretty stiff and sore for a few days, but nothing's broken. You can get dressed. I'll go and tell your partner he can take you home.' She twitched the curtains to one side. 'He's been pacing up and down the waiting room like a caged panther.'

Lily gritted her teeth. 'I don't have a partner.'

The other woman grinned and pushed her glasses up the bridge of her nose. 'I'll let you explain that to him, shall I? He doesn't seem like a listening sort of man to me.'

That doctor was a very astute judge of character, Lily

soon decided as Santiago proceeded to pick up the plastic bag her clothes had been dumped in and marched Lily to the carpark and his waiting car.

'You can rest up at my place,' Santiago instructed as he helped Lily into the passenger seat.

'But I'm not going home with you!' Lily protested.

He slung her a look of total scorn as he turned the ignition. 'Do you imagine even for one second that I'm going to let you stay in Rachel's flat alone?' he asked incredulously. 'You may have conned the medical staff into believing that you're fit enough to go home, but I—'

'I didn't con anyone about anything!' She directed a frustrated grimace at the back of his neck and added, even though she knew there was little chance of him paying any heed to her protestation, 'I *am* well enough.'

'I know you like the sound of your own voice, and I admit it has pleasing qualities when you are not yelling abuse, but we will not discuss the matter farther,' he pronounced calmly.

Lily, who was starting to feel sleepy now the car was moving, couldn't decide if there had been a compliment in there somewhere… 'I'd be much happier on my own, and I'm sure you'd be much happier with me out of your hair,' she continued to argue feebly.

'This is not a matter of what makes me happy. You were driving erratically because I upset you, so I must accept at least part of the responsibility.'

'I keep telling you—the brakes failed.'

'It is late, we are both tired and are liable to say things we might later regret. Tonight you will stay at my house. Tomorrow…'

'Tomorrow you'll have worked off your guilt?'

Briefly his eyes met hers in the rear-view mirror. 'It will take longer.'

CHAPTER THIRTEEN

LILY hadn't expected to, but she'd slept the moment her head had touched the pillow. She had been too exhausted the previous night to take any interest in her surroundings, but this morning she was curious to see where Santiago lived when he was in London.

The place was massive, three storeys and, according to the housekeeper who had presented her with a selection of outfits when she'd brought her morning tea, had a swimming pool and gym in the basement.

'Mr Morais will be in the breakfast room when you're ready. Is there anything special you'd like for breakfast?'

'Thanks, but I'm not hungry.'

'He said you'd say that. Couldn't we tempt you...?'

Santiago could tempt me any day.

'I'll get into trouble if you don't eat.'

The other woman didn't act like someone who thought she was about to lose her job, but for a quiet life Lily relented. 'Scrambled egg and juice would be good.'

The housekeeper beamed approval. 'Excellent.'

It was about half an hour later that Lily, dressed in a silk shirt and classic black trousers, discovered by a process of elimination the breakfast room. She took a deep breath before stepping inside.

Santiago, his long fingers curved around a coffee-cup, turned his head as she walked in. His dark eyes moved up and down the length of her body, but he vouched no opinion on her appearance. 'Did you sleep?'

Lily, who had thought when she'd pirouetted in front of the mirror that she looked rather good, felt quite peeved.

'Yes, thank you.'

As if by magic her breakfast appeared. Lily smiled her thanks and sat down. One eye on the silent man at the end of the table, she broke a warm roll and spread it with butter.

'Would your housekeeper really be in trouble if I didn't have breakfast?'

'I'd sack her without a reference.'

Their eyes met and she grinned. 'You really are a piece of work. I didn't really think you would, you know.'

'You weren't *quite* sure, though, were you, Lily? And you are eating, so it had the desired effect.'

'I'm not anorexic or anything, you know,' she said, putting a forkful of fluffy golden egg into her mouth.

'I realise that.'

'I just forget to eat sometimes. You have a beautiful home.'

'Thank you.'

'Are you here often?'

'Not often enough to call it a home.'

She looked at him curiously. 'What makes a house a home?'

'I prefer to put my faith in people, not brick and mortar.'

'Home is where the heart is?' she suggested.

'Something like that. The clothes—they fit, I see, and, no, they do not belong to an ex-girlfriend. They are my sister's.'

'How did you know I thought…?' she began, and then, meeting his eyes, she blushed and subsided into silence. If he really could read her that well she was in big trouble.

It was a silence he made no attempt to break until she was drinking her second cup of coffee. Then he said in a casual voice, 'You have an appointment with a gynaecologist this morning.'

Lily stiffened. *'What did you say?'*

'If it suits you I think we should leave at ten-thirty to allow for the traffic.'

He was incredible! Did he really think all he had to do was snap his fingers and she would fall in line?

'The only place I am going is home, and you're not coming with me. I'm expected at work tomorrow.' She frowned.

'Under the circumstances it makes sense to get yourself checked out.'

This brought a fresh sparkle of anger to Lily's eyes. 'Frankly I don't give a damn what you think, and even if I did there would be no way I'd be able to see a gynaecologist today.'

'Why not?'

She rolled her eyes. 'Hospital waiting lists?' She supposed his ignorance of the working of the NHS was understandable.

'We are not going to the hospital. Mr Clement has consulting rooms in Harley Street,' he revealed casually. 'His secretary was most helpful.'

'I don't doubt she was,' Lily said bitterly. 'You seem to be under some misguided impression that you have a right to order my life. Let me spell it out for you—I can't afford a private consultation.'

He gave a careless shrug and pulled a folder from the briefcase that was propped up against his chair. 'You don't have to.'

Lily was out of her seat and beside him before he could open it. Breathing hard, she leaned across him until their faces were level. Her voice dropped to a dramatic quiver as she announced, 'I'd prefer to die than accept your charity.'

'You almost did die, because of me.'

'That's ridiculous!' she exclaimed.

'Carrying my child almost killed you.'

She saw it all there in his bleak eyes: self-recrimination; the terrible burden of guilt he was carrying. Everything he was doing, she realized, was about expiating that guilt.

Lily would have drawn back, for his long brown fingers curled over her forearm. The ache inside her chest intensified. She didn't want his guilt. She wanted his love, but that wasn't an offer.

'I was not there then—'

'It wouldn't have made any difference if you had been.'

His shoulders lifted fractionally. 'Maybe…? We will never know, but I am here now, and intend to make amends.'

'And you expect me to be grateful?' She saw a baffled expression filter into his deep-set eyes, but didn't pause long enough to let him respond to her hostile enquiry. 'You're feeling guilty. Well…tough. I didn't ask you to. In fact, I didn't ask for *anything* from you.'

She began to tick off a list on her fingers of the things she *didn't* want from him. 'I don't want your money. I don't want your concern. I don't want you interfering in my life and conspiring with my friends—' She broke off, wincing as the fingers around her arm spasmed.

His grip immediately loosened, and he pulled his hand away. His eyes touched her and then dropped before she could analyse the puzzling expression she had glimpsed in the dark obsidian depths. *'Sorry.'*

She watched through her lashes as he got up and walked over to the window.

'Sorry enough to let me walk through that door and leave me alone for ever?'

Until she had thrown the challenge at him Lily had been convinced this was exactly what she wanted. She would have signed a declaration to that effect.

Now the possibility was out there, perversely she wasn't so sure. It was awfully final. *Final is what I need,* she told herself, irritated by her sudden doubts.

He turned. 'You don't want to be left alone.'

The confident contention was so close to her own thoughts that Lily flushed and responded spikily. 'Sure, I love to have a control freak taking over my life,' she drawled. 'I am quite capable of taking care of myself.'

The muscles around his mouth tightened. 'You have a remarkably casual attitude to your own health,' he condemned harshly.

'Would you prefer I was a hypochondriac?'

'I would prefer you faced facts,' he countered impatiently. 'You've been extremely ill…'

Did he honestly think she needed reminding of the fact?

'You have just endured a slow recovery,' he continued. 'Can you honestly tell me that you're not concerned that yesterday's accident has not in some way compromised that recovery?'

She slung him an exasperated glare. 'Not until you suggested it.' Now of course the uncertainties were going to nag at her.

'Don't let your dislike of me and your stubborn pride prevent you from doing the right and proper thing.'

'You wouldn't know right and proper if you fell over it!'

Her indignant accusation made him laugh.

'Let's work together on this, shall we?'

The casually charismatic smile and the melting-chocolate, coaxing tone alerted her to Santiago's abrupt change of tactics.

'Don't bother with the smoothy charm stuff. I'm immune.' If only, Lily reflected bitterly, this were true. Where Santiago's smiles were concerned she was wide open and vulnerable.

He threw out his hands in a frustrated gesture. 'Fine. I won't waste my time talking to you as though you were a rational human being because clearly you are not. I try and be pleasant and you become abusive.'

'That wasn't pleasant; that was calculating and manipulative,' she contended stubbornly.

'You are the most impossible woman!' The only woman he had ever wanted to wake up next to for the rest of his life. 'Well, calculate this—if you refuse to go willingly to get checked over, I will—'

'*What?*' she cut in scornfully. 'Drag me there kicking and screaming?' An image formed in her head of her slung over his shoulder caveman fashion. Her sensual reaction to the image added an extra layer of venom to her voice as she added, '*I don't think so.*'

Eyes narrowed, nostrils flared, he folded his arms across his chest and looked, Lily had to admit, like a man perfectly capable of slinging a woman over his shoulder and marching through London.

'I don't know why you're making such a big thing of this. You're not going to wear me down, if that's what you think. I've been checked over,' she reminded him. 'Are you suggesting that the staff in Casualty didn't know what they were doing?'

'I'm not saying that,' retorted Santiago impatiently. 'They were obviously dedicated people,' he admitted, thinking of the nurse who, but for his intervention, would have been struck by a drunk.

When the young woman had thanked him he had made a discovery that had appalled him: being physically attacked and verbally abused by drunken patients was considered the norm, not the exception. He had been inclined to encourage his youngest sister's laudable ambition to train as a nurse; now he wasn't so sure that this was such a good idea.

'I am not casting aspersions on their professional ability, but they were tired and overworked. People who are tired make mistakes and miss things.' His eyes burnt with an almost frightening intensity as they swept across her face. She saw the muscles in his brown throat work as he swallowed. 'Have you any idea how damned...breakable you look?'

Lily lifted a self-conscious hand to her neck, and watched his eyes get that dark bleak look that made her heart feel as though it were being squeezed in a vice. 'I did that to you,' Santiago added bitterly.

'Santiago, you haven't done anything to me.'

'I wasn't there when you needed me, but this time I am.'

'What makes you think I need you?'

'Driving around a corner and seeing your car in a ditch.'

Unable to respond to this, she dropped her gaze. Sometimes you had to accept defeat gracefully. 'I'll go and see the damned doctor!' she gritted.

As they approached the Harley Street offices Santiago's phone rang. He fished it out of his pocket and scanned the screen.

His eyes lifted to hers. 'I have to take this.'

'Fine. I don't even know what you're doing here.'

'I'll follow you in.'

'I wish you wouldn't.'

Her childish retort brought a grim smile to his lips. 'It won't take long.'

'Don't hurry on my account.'

Inside, the doctor's rooms were considerably more plush than the NHS outpatients' clinic she had last visited. There was only one other person in the tastefully furnished room she was directed into. The man's face was hidden behind the pages of a broadsheet. She took a seat at the opposite end of the room.

'Can I get you a coffee, tea?' the attentive receptionist asked.

'No, thank you.'

'Mr Clement won't keep you long,' she promised, excusing herself with a smile.

Lily reached for a glossy magazine from the table and began to flip through it.

'Excuse me?'

With a smile she moved her knee and bag to allow the stranger access to the magazines. 'Sorry...' The smile froze on her lips. She gave a gasp of astonishment. 'G-Gordon...?'

'Lily...heavens, this is a surprise...' Her ex-husband cleared his throat.

'Isn't it?' Lily agreed. She wondered if she looked as uncomfortable as he did; she probably did.

'What are you doing here?'

Good question, she thought. *What am I doing here...?* 'This being a gynaecologist's office, shouldn't I be asking you that...?'

'Right, well, if it's private...'

'It is.'

Gordon looked momentarily taken aback, then glanced towards the closed consulting-room door. 'I'm here with Olivia.'

'I thought you might be.'

'She's pregnant.'

Given the meeting was taking place in the waiting room of an obstetrician Lily had been half expecting this, so the impact of hearing that the husband who had said he didn't want children, not *ever*, was about to become a father was not as great as it might have been!

It would seem that Gordon had simply not wanted children with me.

'Congratulations.'

Gordon frowned warily, as though her calm reaction had surprised him.

'We're both very happy about it.'

Did she hear a touch of defensiveness in his voice? Lily realised that she didn't care enough to analyse it. Gordon had stopped having the power to hurt her a long time ago.

'I'm sure you are.' *We never did have a lot to talk about,* she reflected as the uneasy silence stretched. 'You look well. Your new life must suit you.' Gordon's fair, freckled skin had acquired a ruddy hue, he hadn't tanned, but his freckles had joined up.

'It's great,' he enthused. 'I feel like a new man.'

Well, the old one needed some work, she thought and smiled neutrally.

'And you're looking…' The mechanical response faded as his eyes drifted over her. 'Good gracious, Lily, you look *marvelous*,' he said, sounding almost comically amazed. *'Thin.'*

The contrast between her ex-husband's and Santiago's reaction to her new shape brought a wry smile to Lily's lips. It must have been hell for Gordon to be married to a curvy wife, she reflected, feeling surprisingly unemotional about this discovery. Still, he had what he had always wanted now: a skinny wife. She felt sure that Olivia would receive a lot of encouragement after the baby was born to get back her trim figure.

'A bit too thin?'

Gordon looked shocked at the suggestion. 'No, it suits you. I suppose it's after... I was sorry to hear about your miscarriage.'

Lily's expression froze, but Gordon, never being the most perceptive of men, failed to notice the distress suggested by her rigid posture and added with an upbeat smile, 'Still, I expect it was all for the best, as I'm sure you've realised.'

'*The best...?*'

'Well, I'm assuming you didn't intend to get pregnant, but accidents happen,' he conceded magnanimously. 'I should know,' he added under his breath. 'I said to Olivia at the time, good on Lily for going through with it. Given the circumstances a lot of people would have got rid of it.'

It...? Lily gritted her teeth. She wasn't sure now she shouldn't have followed her initial knee-jerk reaction and clobbered him!

'*Circumstances...?*'

'Well, I'm assuming that the father didn't want to know...?' When a stony-faced Lily didn't volunteer any information, Gordon shrugged. 'I have to tell you, when I heard I was shocked. A tacky casual affair just didn't seem like the Lily I knew,' he observed with, as far as she could tell, absolutely no irony. 'I suppose you were on the rebound,' he mused, as though this partly excused her lapse.

'It happened before we split up.'

Gordon's eyes widened. '*You* were unfaithful to *me*?' he gasped, visibly shaken by her confession. 'My God, Lily, how could you?'

Lily was perfectly prepared to take responsibility for her behaviour and own up to her faults, but she wasn't going to take a lecture on morality from her serial adulterer ex-spouse. 'We don't choose to fall in love, but then I don't have to tell you that, do I?'

Their eyes met and he flushed. 'I suppose you think I'm a hypocrite.'

Satisfied she had made her point, Lily let her silence speak for itself.

'I wasn't a perfect husband, I admit that, but whether you like it or not it's different for men. And we both know a child needs a stable home environment and two parents. I know you couldn't have afforded to stay at home or decent childcare… By the way, I've heard the agents have a buyer prepared to pay the asking price on the house…'

'Talk to my solicitor,' she said automatically. 'The child would have had me.'

The sentence felt like a knife sliding between his ribs to the figure framed in the doorway. Upon realizing that the man Lily was chatting to had to be her ex-husband, he'd deliberately not entered the room.

'I'm sure you'd have done your best,' Santiago heard the ex concede pompously.

Dear God, what had she ever seen in him? Santiago wondered. There was no escaping it, the man was, not to put too fine a point on it, a pathetic loser.

He knew that love was not an exact science, but what he had seen and heard had convinced him that this sad individual had nothing to recommend him but a moderately pretty face.

Presumably a face that Lily had liked…maybe still did…?

It was a face that Santiago was discovering he could not look at without longing to rearrange the bland features on it. His hands curled into fists as he fought the impulse to do just that.

'The day would have come the kid would have wanted to know who his dad was, and what would you have told him? No, in the long run it was for the best.'

Lily felt light-headed with anger. That anyone could suggest losing the baby she had wanted so much was 'for the best'—well, she just couldn't let it pass. The irony was this was Gordon's idea of empathy. *How did I ever contemplate spending the rest of my life with this pompous prat?*

She got to her feet and realised that she was shaking. She pressed her interlocked fingers against her chest and took a deep sustaining breath.

Santiago, who had started to move forward into the room, stopped as Lily began to speak.

'I would have told my baby he was much wanted and loved…' Her tremulous voice firmed and got louder as she added, 'I would have told my baby his dad was more of a man than you ever could be!' She stopped and brushed the tears that had spilled onto her cheeks angrily away with the back of her hand.

Gordon, who didn't like tears, looked away. 'Well, really, I don't think personal attacks are called for,' he responded huffily. 'And if this man was so damned great, where is he now?'

'He is right here.'

CHAPTER FOURTEEN

With a startled gasp Lily spun around and collided with a hard breadth of male chest. Her wide blue eyes flew upwards.

'Who says that eavesdroppers hear no good of themselves?'

'S-Santiago.' Before she could get any less articulate he fitted his mouth to hers.

Oh, but it always had been a very good fit, she thought in the split second before an invisible button clicked and her mind switched off. Another one clicked and her hormones switched on.

Oh, boy, did they switch on!

When his head lifted she was breathing as though she'd just run a marathon.

If Gordon hadn't grasped the significance of Santiago's opening gambit, after that kiss she could hardly pass Santiago off as a casual acquaintance. Though she had to concede that the offending kiss might not have been quite so lingering if she hadn't opened her mouth without any coercion.

Her struggle to regain at least a semblance of composure—not easy when she was feverishly shaking from head to toe—suffered a set-back when she allowed herself to think about the stabbing, sensual incursion of his tongue and how her insides had dissolved lustfully. Her eyes went automatically to his mouth and they dissolved all over again.

Show some control, woman! Lily told herself as her

breathing went haywire once more. *This is a public place.* She was peripherally aware of Gordon, standing there with his mouth half open as he gazed at her in the arms of the tall, incredibly good-looking Spaniard.

She made a concerted effort to untangle her thoughts as she forced herself to breath slowly. Clearing her throat, she removed her hands from Santiago's shirt front.

'How long have you been standing there…?' she hissed hoarsely at the man who had her face cradled between his large hands. If Gordon hadn't been watching she would have pulled away.

It didn't even cross her mind that Santiago's comment had been unintentional. He had *meant* for Gordon to know that he had been the father, that they had been lovers.

Why the hell would he do that…?

Still puzzling the motivation behind his behaviour she frowned up into Santiago's lean face. His dark eyes crinkled at the corners as his features relaxed into a lazy, languid smile that made her tummy flip and her knees tremble.

'Long enough to know that I'm finally meeting your ex-husband.' Letting his hands drop from Lily's face, he lifted his dark head and subjected the shorter man to a critical stare before stretching out his hand formally.

If Gordon had picked up on the violent dislike that Santiago was barely repressing, he might have been even slower to take the proffered hand. What he did pick up on, and it made him feel deeply resentful, was Lily's lover's dark, handsome looks, his expensive clothes and his confident, take-control manner.

Gordon, who retained a quaint Victorian assumption that Britain was the centre of the universe, reminded himself that this guy wasn't English. He gave a charitable smile as he complacently observed, 'You're foreign.'

Santiago, who no longer saw any reason to disguise the

fact he didn't like the other man, deliberately allowed his accent to thicken as he replied, 'You're correct. I am not English—I'm...'

A faint, despairing, 'Dear God,' escaped Lily's lips as she heard him outrageously introduce himself.

'Santiago Morais, the Spaniard who stole your wife.'

It seemed to Lily that his wolfish smile challenged Gordon more eloquently than the words.

Suddenly Gordon looked like a man who wished he were somewhere else, and for her part Lily didn't blame him.

Santiago could look daunting when he tried, and he appeared to be trying. What with the arrogant angle of his head, the contemptuous half-smile that pulled lightly at one corner of his fascinating mouth and, most of all, his eyes. He had very expressive eyes and it seemed to Lily that the molten anger gleaming in them at the moment was far in excess of anything Gordon's patronising comment justified.

She could have told him that Gordon didn't mean anything by it, he was just a bit of twit really. The sort of man who thought all women who weren't attracted to him were lesbians and that anything bad that happened to him was someone else's fault. When they had been married that someone had almost always been her!

Contrast was a strange thing, she reflected. Until Santiago had walked into the room Gordon had appeared an above-averagely attractive man. It wasn't that he wasn't attractive; it was that Santiago was *more* attractive.

So I'm not the most objective observer, but... Lily's generous lips curved into a slow, covetous smile as her glance slid over the contours of his lean, powerful body...*he really is gorgeous.*

It wasn't just that Santiago was taller by several inches. Or that he had not an ounce of surplus flesh on his hard, muscled frame and was considerably broader across the shoulders. It wasn't even his startlingly handsome face, charismatic smile or glorious, vibrant colouring. No, it was his effortless air of command, his aura of immutable confidence, the raw male sexuality he projected that drew all eyes, and held them.

Her fingers closed urgently around Santiago's upper arm to draw his attention. It did. His head turned and some of the hostility faded from his face as their eyes connected.

'*Querida…?*'

'You didn't steal me, I gave myself willingly.' *Now why did you think that was a helpful comment?*

Santiago's dark eyes flamed as they moved over her face. 'Yes, you did give,' he agreed. 'And very beautifully.' His voice dropped to a low, intimate drawl that sent a shiver along her raw nerve endings. 'Did I ever say thank you?'

Lily didn't say anything. She had to dig deep into the reserves of her self-control just to keep standing.

'If not…' he ran his thumb caressingly down her smooth cheek '…I'm saying it now. Thank you.'

Gordon, who was standing there watching this intimate interchange, found his voice.

'I had no idea you were with anyone, Lily…'

The hint of reproach in his voice brought a sparkle of annoyance to Lily's eyes as she turned her head. 'That makes us quits. I wasn't meant to know you were with anyone while we were married, which probably makes me very weak for turning the other cheek.'

Gordon flushed at her dry tone, and beside her Santiago looked thoughtful.

This was the first hint he had had of Lily's husband's infidelity.

'And, anyway, I'm not *with* anyone.'

'There is no need to be embarrassed,' Santiago interjected. 'We are both civilised men of the world?' One dark brow elevated, he angled a questioning look at Gordon. 'Is that not so?'

Gordon nodded uneasily. 'Of course.'

'There will be no violence.'

'Don't be too sure of that,' Lily hissed under her breath.

Gordon looked at the athletically built figure of the man who was looming behind Lily and swallowed hard. 'Good grief, no, it's all water under the bridge as far as I'm concerned. And anyway I'm having a baby...that is, my wife...my *present* wife is having a baby.'

His wife appeared at that moment and Lily looked curiously at the woman Gordon had left her for. She had only seen the other woman from a distance before now. She hadn't wanted to—that much hadn't changed, but she had to admit to being curious.

What woman wouldn't want to see what her husband thought was an improvement?

A very tall, slim redhead, she was dressed in a tailored white trouser suit that was cut to minimise the soft swell of her belly. She was deeply tanned and her hair was cut in a short, flattering, feathery style that minimised a prominent square jaw.

For quite a while after she had lost the baby Lily had been unable to look at a pregnant woman or a mother with a baby without feeling a terrible toxic mixture of anger, pain and gnawing loss. Now what she felt had more in common with sadness.

That *had* to be an improvement, didn't it?

'Olivia, look who I met. Lily.'

The other woman came forward showing no signs of the discomfort Lily was sure she would have felt in similar circumstances.

Her manner was confident and composed as she said, 'Hello.'

Lily nodded. She felt quite sorry for the other woman being put in this situation. 'Sorry about this.'

The other woman looked blank. *'Sorry...?'*

'The dumped wife meets mistress thing. It is a bit awkward.'

The redhead looked amused. 'Don't worry your head. I don't feel awkward. Nobody expects a marriage to last for ever these days, do they? And I know yours was over long before me. We're all grown-ups, aren't we? People are far too sentimental about marriage, I think. Treat it like any other contract, that's what I say.' Her smile invited agreement.

Lily, who doubted the other woman would feel quite so 'grown up' if the roles had been reversed, didn't smile back. When Santiago's arm snaked around her waist she allowed herself to be drawn into his side. This was a stressful situation, and she reasoned that she needed all the support she could get—it also felt very good.

'So you think a marriage should be dissolved like a partnership that doesn't work out?' Santiago injected interest into his voice as he gave the woman just enough rope to hang herself.

Lily recognised that the approval in the other woman's eyes wasn't just related to his question. It would be hell to be married to a man who aroused lustful admiration in every woman with a pulse, she thought.

Wow, you really had a lucky escape, the intrusive voice in her head mocked.

'Exactly. I mean love is only for ever in trashy romances.'

She'd never thought she would, but Lily actually started to feel quite sorry for Gordon. 'I like trashy romances,' she felt impelled to protest.

Olivia gave her a look that suggested she wasn't sur-

prised. Lily wondered if Santiago liked tall, athletic redheads and then inwardly mocked herself. *All* men liked tall,
athletic redheads, she thought gloomily. Men were idiots!

'And the accumulated assets of the union divided?'
Santiago persisted.

Lily was amazed that no one else had picked up on the
ironic edge in his voice, and she realised that, far from
being smitten by Olivia, Santiago had taken a dislike to
her. She couldn't help but be a little bit pleased by the
discovery.

'Right down the middle,' she agreed readily. 'California
has it exactly right.'

'A child is hard to split.' Santiago wondered why guys
went for women who looked like boys, especially ones who
had eyes like calculators. Women were meant to be… A
great wave of profound realisation washed over him.
Women were meant to be like Lily.

'Would you stay with a woman just because of a child?'

Beside him Santiago was aware of the tension in Lily's
body stepping up a notch. He looked at the glossy top of
her head just below his shoulder and gently increased the
pressure around her waist.

'Call me old-fashioned, but I'm working on the assumption that I will be in love with the mother of my child.' He
drew Lily even closer.

'The doctor is ready to see you.' The smartly dressed
receptionist's brisk words broke the tension, and Lily grate-
fully extracted herself from Santiago's embrace to follow
the woman down the corridor to the consulting room.

CHAPTER FIFTEEN

'THIS is charming,' Lily admitted as the girl who had taken their order disappeared with a rustle of starched apron.

'I thought you'd like it. My mother always has me bring her and my sisters here for afternoon tea when they visit London.'

'You have sisters…?'

'Two. Carmella is twenty-four. She graduated top of her class from law school.' The pride in his voice was obvious. 'She was married last year.'

'And the other?'

His voice softened. 'Angelica is eighteen.' He frowned. 'She wants to be a nurse. She has her heart set on training in London.'

'And you don't want her to?' Lily speculated, planting her elbows on the table.

'I want her to be happy, but Angel is very quiet and reserved,' he explained. 'The hospital last night…' He appealed to her. 'Tell me, would you want your baby sister to be exposed to that? I admit it was quite an eye-opener to me.'

It was obvious that Santiago took his responsibilities as head of the household very seriously. 'Perhaps you under-estimate her?' Lily suggested quietly.

'Perhaps I do.' Their eyes met, and when Lily analysed the happiness that suddenly suffused her she realised it was directly attributable to the smile in his eyes.

Oh, hell, am I in trouble!

'And there's nothing you can actually do to stop her if that's what she wants to do, is there?'

'You think not?' He sounded amused.

'Well, short of locking her in her room, and that's hardly a long-term solution, is it?'

'If I forbid her she will accede to my wishes.'

Lily stared at him. They obviously occupied two very different worlds.

He arched a brow. 'You find that surprising?'

'I find that medieval—' Lily began, and stopped as the waitress delivered their tea and cakes. The cakes distracted her momentarily from her indignation on behalf of this unknown girl.

'Cream?' asked Santiago.

'Milk.' For some reason she felt the need to support his unknown sister's cause. 'You're only her brother, not her keeper. Why should you have the right to decide what's right?'

'She is young.'

'And female.'

His sculpted lips quivered faintly at her acid insert. 'And being female she might very well change her mind before it becomes a problem.'

Her chin went up at this provocative response. 'Because females are capricious and frivolous?'

A grin spread across his face, making him look, much to Lily's weary dismay, even more devastatingly attractive. He was a doubly dangerous proposition because he wasn't just a pretty face; Santiago had an intellect to match his startling good looks.

'You don't really expect me to answer that, do you?' he asked, sounding amused.

'You don't need to. I already know what you think,' she returned tartly. 'You're a total, unreconstructed male chauvinist.' She levelled her rebellious gaze at him and was shocked by the expression she caught on his face.

'If you knew what I was thinking you wouldn't be...' he began from between clenched teeth.

As Lily watched him breathing hard it was obvious that he had exerted considerable will-power to curtail his sudden and totally uncharacteristic emotional outburst. When he picked up the thread again, or rather *didn't*, the incendiary heat had gone from his eyes and his tone was flat and even.

'Let us just agree to disagree. Angel knows that I have her best interests at heart.'

'That's what all the despots say,' Lily contended, unwilling to be pacified. 'Benevolent or otherwise. I'm just glad I never had a brother like you,' she added crossly.

'I am also glad I am not your brother,' he concurred silkily. Connecting with his eyes, she hastily averted her gaze from the dangerous warmth shimmering in his unblinking regard.

'But if you had had a brother like me perhaps he would have stopped you making a disastrous marriage when you were not much older than Angel,' he observed.

Far from encountering opposition from her grandmother, who had been convinced that marriage was the only true career for a woman, Lily had been positively encouraged to marry.

'If you hang around playing hard to get,' the old lady had cautioned, 'you'll lose him. After all he could have any girl he wanted.'

'You really don't know much about teenage girls, do you?'

His expression hardened. 'I know about men who prey on teenage girls.'

'Gordon didn't "prey" on me.'

'And still you defend him!' Santiago exploded.

Lily stared at him while he swore with fluency and venom.

'Women are stupid!' he said when he had stopped swearing.

Lily knew Santiago didn't mean women, he meant her. As she had pretty much come to the same conclusion herself, though not for the same reasons, she didn't defend herself. Instead she steered the subject in a safer direction.

'Don't you know that teenagers thrive on opposition? Do you have to be so hands-on?' *Cool, skilful hands moving over her damp flesh.* Lily blinked hard to banish the hot, steamy images in her head and willed her expression not to change as she added crankily, 'Couldn't you just sit back, say nothing, and be supportive of your sister's decision?'

He looked at her as though she had lost her mind. 'You think I should be *nice* while she ruins her life?'

'I'll take that as a no, shall I? Perhaps you should try reverse psychology?' she suggested helpfully.

'Rather than say what I honestly think?' The fight not to do so was trying Santiago's patience to its limit.

'Saying what you think isn't always a good idea.'

Santiago's expression didn't change.

Lily looked at the strong, sexily sculpted outline of his lips thinking, *If I told you what I was thinking right now, you'd run a mile. Or maybe you wouldn't run?*

Colour heightened, Lily lowered her eyes. She wasn't sure which possibility scared her most!

Santiago, his expression cloaked, watched as she fiddled with the flowers arranged in a porcelain vase on the table.

'Were you a teenage rebel, Lily?'

Her eyes lifted. She was relieved to see Santiago looked less likely to spontaneously combust at any moment.

'Rebel! Me? No, I wasn't,' she admitted, unaware of the wistful note in her voice.

'Angel isn't a rebel either,' Santiago asserted confidently. He reached across the table and pushed a plate bearing a vast creamy confection towards Lily. 'Eat. It's chocolate.'

Lily took a forkful. 'Some women prefer chocolate to sex. I can see why.' Her eyes lifted from her plate. 'What about you?'

Santiago's long, tapering brown fingers pushed his own plate to one side. 'I prefer sex, and I do not have a sweet tooth.'

Lily had no more control over the colour that flooded into her face than she did the soft, fractured sigh that left her lips.

'So you're just going to sit there and watch me?' she accused, uncomfortably aware of deep-set, disturbing eyes following every move she made, every flicker of expression on her face.

'That was certainly my plan,' he agreed, tilting his chair back as he stretched his long legs out in front of him. 'I enjoy watching you.'

This silky admission did not help Lily relax; it just caused her to miss her mouth.

'You're frowning. Are you still worrying about my sister?' he asked, looking at her soft mouth and feeling hungry. 'As I said, Angel might change her mind so my intervention might not be necessary.'

Lily dabbed her mouth with a napkin and prayed the fine tremor in her fingers wasn't too obvious. 'And then again she might not.'

'True.'

'So what will you do?'

'On past experience I'd say the wrong thing.'

His unexpected frankness made her laugh before she

reapplied herself to the chocolate cake and tried to blank out everything else.

Santiago watched her lay down her fork and looked pleased. 'You enjoyed that. I told you so.'

Lily pushed aside her plate. 'It was very good chocolate cake.'

'I was surprised when you agreed to come here without a fight.'

'I like to keep people guessing.' It made her sound interesting and enigmatic, which she wasn't, but hopefully he wouldn't realise this.

His eyes followed her hand as she added a second spoonful of sugar to her coffee. 'Why did you come?'

Lily stirred her coffee, watching the swirl of the liquid in her cup. 'You asked me,' she reminded him, feeling tense and twitchy because she kept getting increasingly powerful impulses to touch him.

'That is generally enough to make you do the opposite. This unusual compliance,' he confided, 'makes me nervous.'

She slanted a glare at his handsome olive-skinned face. He didn't look nervous; he looked spectacularly gorgeous. She felt an irrational desire to cry and lowered her lashes in a protective screen.

'Well, this is a sort of goodbye, isn't it?' She needed to look to the future, her new life. Santiago was part of the past, and anyway goodbyes were better made on a neutral ground. And there was a limit to how much of a fool she could make of herself in a public place. *I hope.*

Lily smiled, conscious she should be projecting the more upbeat, positive aura of someone who was looking forward to a brand-new start.

His head tilted to one side, though his eyes didn't leave her face. *'It is?'*

Her eyes lifted. 'Please don't act as if you're stupid, Santiago. I know you're not.'

'Why, thank you.'

Lily ignored his sarcastic interjection. 'We both know that the only reason you're hanging around is because you feel guilty. There's no need. You just have an overdeveloped sense of responsibility.' Her eyes slid up from his highly polished handmade shoes to the open neck of his designer shirt. 'Nobody would ever know it to look at you,' she admitted.

'So when you look at me, what do you think?'

That you could make me forget where I end and you begin and I want you to do it again. The sharp inhalation as she gasped for breath made her nostrils flare and her chest lift. 'Sure you want to know?' she taunted weakly.

He smiled and planted his elbows on the table-top. 'I think I can take it,' he said, his eyes trained on her cleavage.

I'm not sure I can.

Lily's smile became even more fixed as she continued to studiously avoid his eyes. 'You look…' she swallowed and exhaled a shaky breath '…not vain and shallow, exactly…'

'I'm relieved,' he came back as dry as dust.

'More dangerous and brooding.'

'*Brooding…?*' he repeated, looking so astounded that any other time she might have laughed.

'Some men spend all their lives trying to look *that* dangerous, brooding, and never get anywhere near.'

'Are you calling me a poseur, Lily?'

'It would be easier if you were.' That was the thing Santiago didn't try at all, she acknowledged despairingly.

'Will you talk sense?' he demanded, running an impatient hand along his firm jawline.

Lily's focus briefly slipped as she indulged her wilful

imagination and visualised doing the same thing. Her fingers flexed as she imagined feeling the rasp of stubble under her fingertips.

'Fine,' she said hoarsely. Blinking, she laid her palms flat on the table-top and fixed him with an earnest gaze. 'Does this make sense to you? I crashed my car...'

She saw anger stir in his eyes. 'Though it wasn't your fault,' he inserted in his flat, cold voice, the one she now recognised he used when he wanted to break things, generally her neck, and yell.

'Does it matter *whose* fault it was?' she asked him in exasperation. 'Anyhow, no matter how you look at it, it wasn't *your* fault, but even if it had been, as you see—' she held her arms out from her sides '—I'm fine.' She pinned a smile on her face to underline the fact.

His dark brows twitched into a straight line and his expression became uncomfortably intense as he studied her face. 'I suppose it wasn't my fault you got pregnant either?'

She gritted her teeth and closed her eyes. 'Not this again. I thought we'd agreed to draw a line under that like rational human beings.'

'You are not rational, and I agreed to nothing.'

Aware that Santiago's raised voice had attracted several curious glances, Lily lowered her own voice to compensate. 'Well, if we didn't, we should have,' she retorted. 'I know you're on some major guilt trip.'

'Naturally, I regret that I was responsible for what you have suffered. What sort of man would I be if I did not feel some guilt?'

She clutched her head between her hands as she let her head flop forward; her hair fell in glossy, concealing bangs around her face.

'If I had had a termination I wouldn't have needed to ask your permission.'

The fine muscles around Santiago's mouth quivered as his jaw tightened. Some of the colour seeped from his olive-toned skin.

'You didn't.'

She had never heard that particular note in his voice before and Lily knew that she never wanted to again. The victim of a sudden and inappropriate wave of tenderness, she was momentarily unable to respond.

'No, I didn't.' Lily had to bite her tongue to stop herself assuring him that this was a course she had never even considered. 'But that was *my* decision. And it was *my* decision to go ahead with the pregnancy. Anything that happened after that was down to me.' She sketched a brief sad smile. 'And fate.'

Her blue eyes met his as she searched in vain for some flicker in those dark, enigmatic depths to show he recognised the point she was desperately trying to get across.

There was nothing.

She gritted her teeth with sheer frustration. 'I take responsibility for my own actions, Santiago. And I am capable of taking care of myself. I realise that you feel you have to go through some sort of penance, but I don't want to be it.'

'*Penance!* That's ridiculous.'

'I don't think so. Why else would you be here with me?' Sniffing, she reached behind her for the bag she had slung over the back of the chair.

Seconds before Lily, Santiago was on his feet looking very tall and *very* angry as he stood the other side of the table glaring at her. A waitress heading in their direction caught the tail-end of his glare and changed direction.

'Maybe I just like looking at you?'

A look of stricken hurt in her eyes, Lily turned her head while she regained control. The irony was he had said *ex-*

actly what she longed to hear. The problem was the comment had been delivered in such a tone of ferocious dislike that even she didn't make the mistake of imagining that he meant it.

From somewhere she dredged a mocking smile. 'Sure, that's *really* likely,' she agreed huskily. 'Considering you've not lost a single opportunity to tell me how dreadful I look. If you want to feel better about yourself, go give something to charity, because I don't need anything from you. I don't need chocolate cake and I don't need you!'

Santiago opened his mouth to assure her the feeling was totally mutual and saw a solitary tear sliding slowly down her pale cheek. He swore softly under his breath, pulled some notes from his wallet and, without even looking, slammed them down on the table.

'Come on. Let's get out of here before someone throws us out,' he said without looking at her.

Robbed of her chance to make a dignified solitary exit, Lily was left with no choice but to follow in his wake.

CHAPTER SIXTEEN

LILY tried to leave Santiago at his car. 'I need to go home.'

Santiago stared at her impatiently. 'We are going home.'

'My home.'

'Get in, Lily, we need to talk.'

'We have talked, Santiago. I'm all talked out.' She shook her head sadly from side to side. 'The truth is, talking isn't going to change anything. Let me spell it out for you: I don't need rescuing. You feel guilty. You're one of the good guys. I understand that. It might make you feel better to act as my protector, but quite frankly being around you only reminds me of things I'd prefer to forget.'

His head reared back as though she had struck him. Shock registered in his face, then slowly his lean features settled into a blank mask.

'You look at me and think of losing the baby.' He met her eyes and gave a bleak smile that made Lily's tender heart ache. 'I must admit I had not thought of that.'

Neither did I until ten seconds ago, she thought, and felt wretched. She stuffed her hands into her pockets to stop herself reaching out to him. *This is the right thing to do,* she told herself. *In the long run it will be less painful. Guilt is no basis for any sort of relationship, and even though he hasn't got around to it yet I'm pretty sure that's what he's going to suggest.*

And if he did she wasn't sure she would have the strength to say no.

'Get in,' he said tersely. 'And I will drive you home.'

Just like that. If he really cared he would have put up some sort of fight. 'To Devon?'

'Certainly to Devon.' He frowned, then added, 'Where is Devon? And I thought you lived with Rachel now?'

She shook her head. 'God, this is stupid. I can catch the train.'

'I have driven across several continents. I think I can find my way to Devon.' Lily watched him run his hand along his jaw; she had never heard him sound so tired before. 'Get in, Lily.'

It was the worrying note of exhaustion in his voice that made her stop arguing. 'Thank you.'

They travelled in silence, the rain, grey, depressing sheets of it, began to fall before they had even left the city. By the time they got on the motorway the visibility was abysmal and the traffic heavy. Then, twenty miles on, the traffic came to a complete standstill.

'Accident…?' she suggested tentatively, after they had moved ten feet in half an hour.

'It would seem likely.'

Lily pushed her hair back from her brow and wound down the window, which let in fumes and rain. 'How can you be so calm?' So far he had not even drummed his fingers on the dashboard, and she felt like tearing her hair out. Listening to him rant and swear would be preferable to the nerve-shredding silence.

'There is no point stressing over things that are outside your control. Would you like to listen to the radio or some music?'

'You're not human.'

He turned his head. 'I'll take that as a no, shall I?'

Lily took a map from the glove compartment just as the traffic started creeping forward at a snail's pace. 'I thought so,' she said, after she had located the right page. 'There's an exit in about a quarter of a mile.' She traced a route along minor roads with her fingers. 'It's less direct, but it should be faster than this.'

'Building a new motorway would be faster than this,' he said, indicating to manoeuvre into the inside lane.

About half an hour later, after several miles of incident-free driving on a minor road, they hit the first diversion sign. Santiago slowed as a policeman approached and wound down the window as he came to a stop.

'Flash floods. The road ahead is closed, sir. If you follow the diversion signs it'll get you back on the motorway.'

'I don't believe this,' Lily groaned under her breath. She turned to Santiago. 'What are you going to do?'

He scanned her pale face and made a rapid mental calculation. 'We're going back.'

'What?'

'You're clearly exhausted, and I'm not getting any younger while I drive around the west country. It will be quicker to go back to London than go on, unless you prefer to stop overnight in a hotel here? The choice is yours, but first—' he pulled into the forecourt of a roadside pub '—I need to ask you something.'

Lily looked across at him. Santiago didn't quite meet her eyes. Her brow furrowed into a quizzical frown.

'You don't usually find it difficult to say what's on your mind, Santiago.'

'This is a difficult thing to ask,' he continued. 'I need to know if the complications of the birth and surgery affected your fertility. Will you be able to have more children?'

The question was so totally unexpected that the breath snagged in her throat. Almost immediately her lashes lowered in a protective screen over her eyes. When her head came up her expression was as devoid of emotion as her voice.

'I rather think that's my business, don't you?'

'I am only…'

She lifted her hand to silence him. 'The *only* person it might concern would be the person I intended spending the rest of my life with.' The muscles along her delicate jaw quivered. 'And that's not you, is it? I expect *your* wife when you eventually take one, poor woman, will need to supply a medical certificate to certify she is good breeding stock. You and your precious family pride,' she sneered. 'I suppose it's understandable if you have an aristocratic bloodline that stretches back to the year dot.'

A look of frustration settled on his dark saturnine features as he studied her expression. *'Lily…?'* His long brown fingers touched her wrist and she flinched and pulled her hand away as though burnt.

'If I say I can't have children, what are you going to do, Santiago?' Inside her tight chest her heart was hammering; for some reason she was so angry she felt light-headed.

'How are you going to fix it?' She saw him flinch and told herself she didn't care. 'Offer me money? How much is it worth, do you think? Isn't that what men like you usually do—throw money at a problem until it goes away? Well, I don't want your guilt money. And, just for the record, I have no intention of remarrying.' *Like he actually cares, Lily.*

'That would, I think, be a pity,' he said quietly.

'But if I did, it wouldn't be to a man who thought of me as a baby machine.' Lily didn't know why it was, but around Santiago she seemed to regress to childish retorts.

Rather than the annoyance she had anticipated there was curiosity and something else she couldn't put a name to in his face as he asked, 'You really think that is what I want in a wife?'

'I can't say I've given any thought to what you might

want in a wife,' she declared, and then almost immediately contradicted herself by adding, 'Oh, I'm sure she'd have to be talented, beautiful. And probably blonde.' She tossed her head.

Santiago's eyes followed her hair as it bounced and settled back around her shoulders. 'No,' he said, smiling in a way that made her stomach muscles quiver. 'My preference is for brunettes.'

'Am I meant to be flattered?' Lily knew what she definitely meant *not* to be, and that was turned on. Turned on to the extent that she was only a whisper away from salivating.

Very conscious of his dark, smouldering gaze lingering on her lips, she attempted a scornful laugh, but all that emerged was a hoarse whimper.

Pathetic, Lily, she told herself.

'And for the record, my preference is for men who don't make personal comments.'

'I don't have an aristocratic bloodline,' he said, still looking at her mouth.

'Sure, you're a regular man of the people.'

'And I cannot trace my family back to…"the year dot".'

'Your family tree isn't actually something I stay awake at nights wondering about.' No, just his voice, and hands, his eyes and the way he had of turning his head to one side when he was about to ask a question…

'I have.'

'You have what?'

'I have stayed awake nights wondering about my family tree. You see, I actually have no idea who my biological parents were.'

Lily's jaw literally dropped. She blinked at him, not quite sure of what she'd heard. 'Your "biological" parents…?'

The frown between her brows deepened. 'What are you saying? *Biological...?*'

'I'm saying that I was adopted.'

'*You* were adopted?' She shook her head. 'No, that can't be right?'

His sensual, dark, delectably velvety eyes shimmered with emotions she couldn't even begin to decipher as they connected with her own.

'It was not something my parents advertised,' he admitted drily. The upward curve of his lips was self-derisive as he added, 'Not even to me.'

She looked at him in horror as the significance of his words sunk in. 'They didn't tell you...?'

'I was going through my father's papers after his death when I came across the paperwork.'

'Oh.' Lily just couldn't begin to imagine how devastating that must have been.

He scanned her horrified face, a half-smile on his lips. 'Be careful, Lily, your empathy is showing.'

'Empathy! I should think so! You found out you were adopted by accident.' She unfastened her seat belt and thought angrily about his parents. 'It must have been a...' She stopped, unable to come up with anything that wasn't totally trite.

'I was shocked,' he admitted.

She flashed him an incredulous look. '*Shocked...*' she repeated. *Oh, well,* she thought, *I suppose that is one way to describe having your life shaken to its foundations. A discovery like that would make your average person question a lot of things they had taken for granted before...things like who they were!*

She slid a searching look at Santiago; he didn't look like a man who had an identity crisis. He looked like a man who was totally at ease with who he was.

'Have you tried…tried to find your birth mother?' She caught him looking at her strangely and added awkwardly, 'I only ask because I've heard that a lot of people feel the need to discover their birth parents.'

'That would be difficult as I was adopted in Argentina.'

'Argentina!'

'My mother has family there. My parents tried for children for some years. Adoption was something of a last resort and they were very discreet. They went to stay with relatives in Argentina. My father came home and later my mother returned with me. Even when I found the adoption documents she initially denied it. Finally she broke down and admitted it.'

Lily listened with growing astonishment to his calm recitation. 'You know, you're so good at hiding your feelings that some people probably think you don't have any.'

His eyes flickered her way. 'But not you?'

'You forget I've seen you lose your temper—on more than one occasion,' she added drily. 'I just don't understand why it was a secret. They must have realised you would find out eventually.'

He shrugged. 'Maybe they didn't think that far ahead.'

She just couldn't believe he was as relaxed as he appeared. 'Weren't you angry?'

'Actually it explained a lot of things.'

'Such as?'

'My relationship with my father.'

'Which wasn't good,' she speculated.

'Which wasn't good,' he agreed calmly. 'My father told me from an early age that I was a disappointment to him. He continually tried to undermine me. I suppose my early life was defined by my attempts to prove him wrong. It was a long time before I realised that that wasn't possible.'

Lily literally bounced in her seat as her feelings of indignation threatened to overcome her. 'Well, he was wrong,' she cried, brushing an angry tear from her cheek. 'And if he was here I'd tell him so.'

His eyes moved across her face. 'I believe you would; you're quite a tigress.'

'And I just think it was stupid not to tell you from the start. If I ever adopted a child I wouldn't make a secret of it.'

'You didn't know my father.' He gave an ironic smile. 'But then neither did I. You have to understand that, to him, not being able to produce an heir was a source of intense shame. I was a reminder of his failure.' He twisted around in his seat and angled a questioning look at her face. 'And is it likely that you would one day adopt a child, Lily?'

Lily's shoulders tensed, then relaxed. Why not put him out of his misery? 'If I did it wouldn't be because I couldn't have one of my own.'

It was only when he relaxed that Lily appreciated just how much her reply had meant to him.

'You are sure?'

'It was one of the things that the doctors made a point of telling me,' she recalled, unaware of the bleak expression that had settled on her face as her thoughts drifted back to that black period. 'They seemed to think it would be a comfort to me.' Her smile was bitter. 'But I didn't want another baby. I wanted *my* baby.'

Her eyes lifted and the expression in his dark eyes made her stiffen. The one thing she didn't want was his pity.

'So you can put your hair shirt back in mothballs,' she snapped.

He looked at her for a moment in silence. 'Why are you angry with me?'

Damn him and his spooky perception! 'I'm not angry with you,' she snapped crankily.

'Then what are you?'

'I'm...I'm *mad* with you because you're only around because you feel guilty.' *I want you to be around because you want to be with me. I want you to feel as if your life is empty without me in it!* Her eyes were filled with a helpless longing as they moved across his lean face.

I want you to feel the way I do.

Blinking back tears, she turned her head away, mumbling, 'Well, like I've already said, I'm not some pathetic charity case.'

'I'm around because your mouth is sweet and hot and I'm hoping at some point to get to taste you again. How the hell can you think I'm just around because I feel guilty after what happened between us at Dan's cottage?' he demanded.

Sniffing, Lily slowly turned her head. *'Seriously...?'*

He looked into her wary eyes. 'Does it look like I'm not serious? Look, I'm willing to walk away if looking at me brings back a pain I can't even begin to imagine. But why do you think I took you to bed? Out of some weird sense of duty?'

'I suppose I might have read the situation wrongly?'

He heaved an enormous sigh and looked relieved. 'Well, thank God for that. My motivation is far less noble.'

'It is?'

He nodded and the hungry gleam in his eyes, the one that made her feel breathless, got more pronounced. 'I can't look at you without imagining you naked. I can't think about you without wanting to be inside you.' There was a dangerous gleam in his eyes as he added firmly, 'Not noble.'

This was good, she told herself. Love would be better.

She gave a ghost of a grin—but she could settle for lust. It was miles better than the alternative, which was never kissing Santiago again. No, she would definitely settle.

'Not noble, but…exciting.'

He looked into her face and swallowed. 'I think we should continue where we left off.'

'But what about what happened between us in Spain?'

With a frustrated sigh, he pushed his dark head into the upholstered seat. 'Fine, let's get this out of the way. I now know that your husband was a total bastard who cheated on you.'

Her eyes flickered in surprise. 'In a nutshell, yes, but—'

'A nutshell works for me,' he promised. He closed his eyes and covered the lower part of his face with his hands. 'Have you any idea what the scent of your skin is doing to me?'

Lily would have loved to have him describe this in detail, but she really needed to clear the air. 'It wasn't all Gordon's fault.'

Santiago's hands fell away. 'You're defending him?'

'I'm trying to be fair. He had flings, because he said, and please don't laugh, he said I didn't understand him.'

'The man is a complete fool!' Santiago observed contemptuously.

'Yes, I know that *now*, but at the time I didn't. I think habit was the only thing holding us together by the end. There had been signs, lots of them,' she recalled. 'But I just didn't want to admit that I'd failed. If I'd been stronger I'd have ended it a lot earlier,' she admitted. 'So I am partially responsible.'

'The Spanish holiday…' She shot him a sideways look and saw he was listening intently. 'It was meant to be a fresh start, a second honeymoon. Only he got called away

at the airport. He said he'd follow on, but he didn't.' She
shook her head. 'I didn't set out to lie to anyone,' she told
him earnestly. 'I was going to tell you the truth about being
married, but then it was too late and…'

He leaned across and laid a finger to her lips. 'I can see
now how it happened.'

A twinkle appeared in her eyes. 'You're just saying that
so that you can kiss me,' she teased.

He trailed a languid finger down her cheek. 'I can see
that you will be hard to fool.'

He began to edge towards her and Lily pulled back.
'About the kissing…'

'You have a problem with the way I kiss?'

'Not the kissing, only the stopping,' she admitted. Then,
correctly anticipating that Santiago was about to pull her
into his arms, and knowing that she wouldn't be able to
think, let alone talk, rationally when she got there, she
added quickly, 'I was thinking, if we're going to be…an
item…?'

He placed a hand on her thigh. 'That is one way of putting it,' he agreed, smiling as he felt a shiver run through
her body.

'Then maybe we should do things properly this time?'

He stilled. '"Properly"…?' he echoed. 'Last time felt
faulty to you…?'

She flushed and felt her nipples harden. 'The sex is not
a problem.'

One dark brow elevated. 'Do you think you could work
on the enthusiasm for the sake of my ego?'

'Your ego could withstand an earthquake,' she contended
with a quick nervous laugh. 'I'm just trying not to think of
sex with you, because when I do my mind turns to mush.
And I want to say this.'

'"Mush"?'

She nodded. 'There's no need to look so smug,' she choked.

He adopted a grave expression. 'Fine, I am listening.'

'I just thought we could go on dates…the theatre…things like that.'

Or we could just go to bed. 'Anything you like. What food do you like—Chinese, French, Thai…?'

'I'm serious, Santiago.'

Eyes narrowed, he studied her face. 'Is this some sort of test? You want to know if I just want you for your body. Do you want me to love you for your mind?'

She didn't try to laugh, because she knew she wouldn't be able to pull it off. 'I *know* you only want me for my body.'

About to speak, Santiago closed his mouth when she added quickly, 'Which is fine. I want you for your body too. Only I thought it might be nice to talk, and things, sometimes, otherwise…' she flushed and her eyes dropped '…I'd feel like your mistress. I'm not really mistress material.'

She looked at him, frowning as she remained unable to interpret his dark stare.

'Fine, you want to date, we will date.' He went to turn the ignition, then changed his mind and turned back to her. 'I thought we had been talking. And just how many people do you think I have discussed the circumstances of my birth with? I'll tell you, shall I? Nobody.'

Before she had chance to consider this startling piece of information, he added, 'It is getting late. We should start back.'

Lily glanced over at the pub, which was now illuminated by a garish set of multicoloured lights. 'We could stay there. It doesn't look busy. Probably the weather.'

Santiago looked at the building with an expression of fastidious distaste. 'Or the peeling paintwork?'

'Don't be such a snob,' she chided. 'I'm sure it's lovely inside.'

'Your optimism is admirable.'

She gave a reluctant smile. 'All right, it does look a bit tatty, but do you really want to drive all the way back?'

'No,' he admitted. 'That is not my first call.' A thoughtful expression slid into his eyes as he looked at the building. 'This dating, Lily—how far do you want to take it?'

'How do you mean?'

'I mean do you want single rooms?'

'You mean…' A look of horror spread across her face. 'God, no,' she gasped. 'I didn't mean that at all.'

He smiled. 'In that case I think we should by all means spend the night in this delightful establishment.'

CHAPTER SEVENTEEN

LILY spent most of the week packing and looking for somewhere to rent that was reasonably close to work. There was no possibility of buying in a town where the property prices had been artificially inflated by the influx of people buying second homes close to the sea. And the rental market did not offer too much choice—not on her limited budget anyway.

But by the end of the week she had signed a lease on a tiny bedsit. It was cramped, but if you stood on a chair and looked through the skylight in the bathroom you could just see the sea. When the agent had assured her with no trace of irony that a sea view was a real selling point she had tried not to laugh.

She was really trying to be upbeat and put a positive slant on the whole downsizing thing, but it was difficult. The future was still a question mark, but one good thing was the library had offered her a full-time post. The extra money would make life a lot easier.

She looked around at the packing cases in the living room, and thought, *Shouldn't I feel something? This was my home for most of my adult life.* Maybe Santiago had been right, she reflected. Maybe it did take more than bricks and mortar to make a home.

Santiago… She sighed as his lean face materialised in her mind. In theory she should not have had time to miss him; in reality she had thought about something he had said, or did, or just the sound of his voice, just about every minute of the day. Twice he had rung her during that week, and on each occasion the conversation had been strained and awkward. And after she had put the phone down she had cried her eyes out.

She could acknowledge that it was a pathetic way for a grown woman to behave, but she couldn't stop missing him so much it hurt. As she locked the door for the last time and headed for the station it was the thought of seeing him again that gave her step a new sense of urgency as she carried her case to the London-bound train.

'Why are we doing this?' she asked as the taxi drew up outside the restaurant.

She had arrived in London dizzy with anticipation. The rather reserved reception she had received had left her feeling distinctly deflated. Then, instead of whisking her off to bed, Santiago had said he was taking her out to dinner and then a show—*a show, for God's sake*!

Maybe he had gone off her already?

Santiago, who was saying something to the cab driver, turned his head. 'Doing what?'

'What are we doing here?'

'You prefer another restaurant? This place comes highly recommended and tables here are like gold-dust since they got the second Michelin star, but if you prefer some place else, fine.'

'I *mean* why are we here at all? It's pretty obvious you don't want to be.'

'I don't know what you mean.'

'Not looking at me I can take, limited conversation I can take, but it would be nice to get more than a grunt in response to a question. Since it's quite obvious you'd prefer to be somewhere else I wonder what we're doing here at all.'

Something flashed in his eyes. 'It is true I would prefer to be some place else.'

Lily's throat tightened. She would have died rather than show him how much his admission hurt. Through a miasma of misery she heard him add angrily, 'But you wanted this.'

'I wanted what?' *I wanted to be ignored and insulted…?*

'You wanted to take things slowly…'

'Yes…' she said, not seeing where he was going with this.

'A date, you said,' he reminded her through clenched teeth. 'This is a date.'

Lily stared at him. 'You think that I want this?'

There was a thunderstruck silence. 'Are you saying you don't?'

She shook her head. 'You said that there was somewhere else you would prefer to be,' she said. 'Where's that?'

If she was wrong, if he said with someone who didn't bore him silly, she was going to feel pretty stupid. No, actually, she was going to feel much worse than that.

'I would prefer to be naked in bed with you.'

A choking sound was heard from the front seat, but neither of the occupants of the back seat noticed.

'Me too,' said Lily.

'Well, why didn't you say so sooner?' Santiago tapped on the glass partition. 'Change of plan.' He leaned back in the seat and loosened his tie. His dark eyes moved over Lily and her stomach flipped. 'Come here…'

Lily scooted across the intervening inches and placed her hands behind his dark head. 'Will this do?'

'*Dios…!*' he breathed brokenly as she pressed her soft breasts against his chest.

'Santiago…you remember what I said about not being mistress material?'

He looked at her mouth, soft pink and inviting, and nodded. 'I do…it doesn't matter,' he promised.

'No, it doesn't,' she agreed, 'because I've changed my mind.'

'You want to be my mistress?'

'I'll be anything you want me to be. I don't care so long as I'm with you.' Tears sprang to her eyes. 'The last few days without you have been hell,' she confessed.

A huge silent sigh shuddered through his body as he took her face between his hands. 'We will discuss your official title later,' he promised, rubbing his thumb along the trembling outline of her lips. 'Because right now if I don't kiss you I will go mad.'

'Oh, me too!'

Ten minutes later Santiago opened the door of the Georgian town house and they almost fell into the hallway. Still kissing the woman in his arms, he began to fight his way out of his jacket. Once it was gone he slid his hands into her hair, twisting his fingers into the shiny mesh and tilting her head back to expose the length of her pale neck.

Their lips parted as they both gasped for air. Santiago looked from her half-closed blue eyes to her deliciously pouting lips and groaned.

'You are driving me crazy. Do you know that?'

'*I am?*' Lily said

His smouldering eyes zoned in on her parted pink lips. 'I'm on my way to being certifiable.'

She lifted a hand to his cheek and ran her finger down the hard, strong curve of his jaw, feeling the rough growth of beard that gave him a wildly attractive, piratical air.

Head thrown back, she looked up at him through her lashes. 'Is there anything I can do to help?'

Santiago swallowed and his tense grin grew even more wolfish and hungry. 'What did you have in mind?'

'I'm open to suggestions.' At that moment Lily couldn't

think of any request he might make that she would deny him. Anticipation made her senses swim.

'*Querida!*' he breathed, wiping the beads of sweat from his forehead with the back of his hand. The primal hunger coursing through his veins made it hard to think of anything but having her softness underneath him, then she nibbled his neck and his eyes flickered open. Looking into her sweetly flushed face, he grabbed both her hands in one of his and held them lightly behind her back.

'This is crazy,' she said as he bit the side of her mouth.

'Do you like crazy?'

'Oh, yes...'

Lily's feet barely touched the ground until her back made contact with the wall. Breathing hard, she stood there with her hands now pinioned against either side of her face and her passion-glazed eyes lifted to the dark, lean face of the man whose body, every rock-hard, sinfully delicious inch of it, was plastered up against hers.

His mouth brushed softly against hers and she closed her eyes and shivered.

'Have you the *faintest* idea how much I want you?' he demanded thickly.

His words jolted through her body like a mild-electric shock. Her lips quivered faintly as her eyelids half lifted. Through the sweep of her lashes she tried to focus, but his face was so close his features were just a dark blur.

She swallowed. 'Quite a lot?' she suggested.

'*Quite a lot...*' he repeated slowly.

She started to nod, and stopped as his tongue began to trace the outline of her full, quivering lower lip. 'I'm never going to let you out of my sight for this long again.'

Neither heard the drawing-room door swing open, or registered the light that spilt out into the hallway from that room.

CHAPTER EIGHTEEN

'GOOD evening, Santiago.'

Against her, Lily felt Santiago's warm body stiffen and lift from her own. The quarter-inch of air between them made her feel suddenly icily cold and irrationally bereft.

Eyes closed tight, he exhaled a ragged breath. Swearing softly and fluently under his breath did little to relieve the frustration that coursed through his veins. Families, he decided, were totally overrated, especially when they turned up uninvited at crucial moments in a man's life.

As his head lifted Lily's eyes meshed with his for a moment. She was too mortified at finding herself in this cringingly embarrassing position to be capable of reading the message in his eyes. Maybe Santiago recognised this because just before he turned away from her he said in a rough velvet voice meant for her ears alone, 'Don't move, *querida.*'

If Lily hadn't been literally paralysed with embarrassment she would have had no problem ignoring this husky instruction, sexy endearment or no sexy endearment, and getting the hell out of there! As it was it took her thirty seconds before she lowered her hands from the wall; running at that point was not a serious option.

'What are you doing here, Mother?' he asked, sounding composed but seriously irritated.

Lily, who wanted quite badly for the floor to open up and swallow her, was deeply envious of his composure. Other than the dark lines of colour scoring the high angles of his cheekbones and the ruffled condition of his normally sleek sable hair, he looked relaxed.

Santiago's mother! Lily was briefly diverted from her own misery as she looked across at the older, dark-haired woman. The slim figure standing there didn't look much like the mental image of scary matriarch Lily had nursed. For a start, she didn't look nearly old enough.

Patricia arched a delicate eyebrow, but her serene smile didn't waver at her son's accusing tone. 'When you weren't at the airport to pick me up we got a taxi,' she explained calmly.

Santiago dragged a hand through his dark hair and frowned. His thoughts, not totally committed to this conversation, kept straying back to moments before when Lily had melted into his arms, all sweet softness and heat. He thought about the way she had shuddered from head to toe, the fine muscles just under the surface of her silky skin contracting as he had laid his fingers on the bare skin of her thigh. It took all the will-power at his disposal to prevent himself grabbing her again and burying his face between her breasts.

He inhaled and cleared his throat.

'Airport…?' he snapped abruptly.

'It slipped your mind, no doubt?' A smile quivered on Patricia Morais's lips as her dark eyes moved from her son's face to that of the young woman at her son's side. 'Are you not going to introduce me to your friend, or is this not a good time?'

The older woman's dark almond-shaped eyes flickered towards Lily, who was standing there with her lace-edged pink camisole and a lot of flesh on show. Moments before her skin had been flushed with passion; now it was mortification that produced the heat that made Lily's cheeks burn. Her fingers shook as she dragged her shirt together and tried to fasten the buttons.

The only discernible expression on Santiago's mother's face was mild curiosity, but of course it wasn't hard for Lily to imagine what the elegant older woman was thinking. Probably wondering where her playboy son had picked up this one.

Comparing me to the others…? I wonder how I score?

Lily suddenly felt as wretchedly cheap as she was sure the other woman thought her.

Santiago gritted his teeth and tucked his own shirt back into his trousers. 'No, it damn well isn't a good time.'

'I thought it might not be.' As his mother spoke a young woman with big dreamy dark eyes and a serious expression appeared at her shoulder.

Lily saw that the girl's heart-shaped face was attractively framed by a barely tamed mass of dark curls. She had a natural pout and her golden Mediterranean skin glowed with youth and vibrance.

She was quite breathtakingly beautiful.

'Is Santiago here *finally*?' There was no trace of accent in her loud voice.

Lily's spirits took a predictable nosedive. A beautiful girl asking for…no, *demanding* Santiago. Why should this surprise me? she asked herself sardonically.

The brunette's voice dropped to a more acceptable level as she unplugged the earphones from her ears and asked cheerfully, 'What's his excuse for leaving us stranded? This ought to be good,' she anticipated.

She saw Lily and stopped. Her big eyes widened as they turned in enquiry first to her, then Santiago and the older woman.

'Angel! Dear God, you as well?' Santiago demanded in

a less-than-welcoming tone that drew an amused grin from the dark-haired beauty.

'Hello, big brother. I'm glad to see you too,' she quipped drily. 'I would be here, wouldn't I?'

He shook his head as his normal acute mental capability failed him. 'Would you?' he responded with caution.

'I'm here for my interview on Friday, for the nursing degree.' The way she studied her brother's face, with her head tilted a little to one side, reminded Lily of Santiago. 'You'd forgotten,' she concluded.

'I had not forgotten,' Santiago contended. 'It had simply temporarily slipped my mind.'

The last remnants of gravity vanished from Angel's face as she gave an impish grin. 'Which is an entirely different thing.' She laughed a little at her brother's expression and stepped forward, her hand outstretched to Lily. 'I'm Angel, Santiago's sister.' She cast a sideways glance at her brother. 'What have you done with him?'

'Not now, Angel. I'll talk to you later.' He took a step forward, interposing his big body between Lily and his family.

Lily's vision misted; the action seemed painfully symbolic to her. When he said, 'Not now' what he really meant was, *Not ever*! It was obvious that the last thing Santiago wanted to do was introduce her to his family. She blinked and swallowed past the emotional constriction in her throat.

Get used to it, Lily. There's going to be a lot of this. The reality of what she was doing suddenly hit her like a truck-load of bricks.

She told herself it wasn't reasonable to feel hurt, but then when did loving someone have anything to do with reason? It wasn't as if Santiago had lied at any point to her. She had entered into this knowing that he didn't love her—knowing that he wasn't able to return her feelings.

The bottom line was she had been willing to take what she could get and she didn't regret her decision, but she was starting to appreciate how hard that was going to be.

As she turned she didn't have the faintest idea where she was going—she just knew she had to escape this situation before she did something really daft like cry.

'If you'll excuse me,' she mumbled, sure that he would.

She was wrong.

'No, I will not excuse you,' Santiago announced, in a tone that made the female members of his family stare in amazement at him.

'I thought you were embarrassed by my presence.'

His glittering midnight eyes swept across her pale-as-paper face; the tears standing out in her eyes made him frown. 'Then you thought wrong, and not for the first time. For the record, you're not going anywhere. You're staying right here with me.'

Lily's chin went up in response to his autocratic pronouncement. Emotional basket case or not, she wasn't going to let him get away with talking to her like that. She might have no pride where he was concerned, but she wasn't a doormat.

'Are you telling me, or asking me?'

His mobile lips quivered and some of the severity died from his face as the lines around his eyes deepened. 'Would it make any difference?'

Their eyes meshed. His were dark and warm and so tender that for a moment she couldn't get her breath.

Lily thought about what they'd be doing now if his mother hadn't walked in and her hand went to her neck where her skin prickled hot and sticky.

'You're incredibly bossy,' she charged gruffly.

'It is part of my charm,' he claimed.

Lily looked into his face and thought, *I love you so much*

it hurts. 'Your problem is you've started believing your own press releases,' she taunted, trying to sound amused and just not getting there at all.

'Do I have press releases?'

Lily wasn't sure whether he was serious. 'Don't you know?'

'Well, if I do, in future you shall have control over all press releases. That should keep my ego from spiralling out of control,' he added with an ironic twist of his lips.

'That would be nepotism.'

He shrugged. 'I don't have a problem with that.'

'The people who work for you might if you invented a job for your mistress.' She didn't have the faintest intention of working for him, but she felt this was something that needed saying.

'What did you say?'

Lily immediately realised why he looked so furious. He didn't want her advertising their relationship in front of his mother and sister, which was pretty unfair considering he had initiated the conversation in the first place.

'She's your mistress?'

With a curse Santiago rounded angrily on the round-eyed teenager. 'No, she is not!'

'Keep your hair on. I was only asking.'

'If I'm not your mistress, what am I?'

Before Santiago could respond to this challenge Patricia Morais, who had been watching the interchange, released a soft cry. 'Goodness, I know who you are.'

Glad someone does, Lily thought, unable to tear her eyes from Santiago's face.

'You're the girl Santiago told me he was going to marry. A year ago…*August.* It was my birthday,' she recalled. 'So I remember the date exactly. You rang, Santiago. It was after midnight and you said you couldn't come to my birthday celebrations because you'd met the girl you were going to marry.' She released a reminiscent laugh. 'At first I thought you'd been drinking.'

Santiago didn't confirm or deny his mother's words; he didn't even turn his head. His dark, implacable gaze remained trained unblinkingly on Lily's shocked face.

'*Marry…?*' Lily, her smooth brow furrowed, shook her head.

'It is her, isn't it?'

'You told your mother you were going to marry me a year ago?' Lily's head swung slowly from side to side as she tried to make sense of this information. 'No, that can't be right.'

She saw something move behind Santiago's dark eyes before his lashes came down in a concealing screen. '*Why?*' The single word fell heavily into the charged atmosphere.

Lily looked at Santiago, who was nursing his dark head between his hands. 'Because in August we'd only just met.'

His head lifted; the pain in his eyes shocked Lily. 'And how long does it take to fall in love?'

Somewhere in the distance Lily heard Angel squeal. 'That's *so* romantic!'

Santiago tore his eyes briefly from Lily's face to beg of his mother, 'Will you get that girl out of here?'

'I'm not a girl!' his sister protested indignantly. 'Does this mean I'm finally going to get to be a bridesmaid?'

After the sound of the door slamming, there was silence for a full sixty seconds.

Lily, whose heart was trying to climb out of her chest, trained her eyes on the floor. 'You're not in love with me,' Lily said in a manner that invited contradiction.

A nerve clenched in Santiago's lean cheek. 'Are you asking me or telling me?' he rasped huskily.

She turned her head away from him and caught a glimpse

of herself in a mirror. The light in the brightly lit hall was pretty unforgiving and she looked quite desperately pale. Her eyes, which seemed to fill half of her face, held a feverish glitter.

'I don't know what I'm doing. I don't know what I'm saying,' she confessed weakly. Just when she had come to the conclusion she knew nothing at all, she remembered something she did know. It actually seemed like the only constant in her turbulent life just now. For once she wasn't thinking of the consequences as she blurted out, 'I love you, though; I know that much.' A wave of fatigue swept over her so intense she sought the lower step of the elegant, sweeping staircase and sat down without even looking at him.

Her eyes were trained on her shoes as she heard his soft tread on the marble floor. The brief contact as his thigh lightly touched hers sent a hot tingle through her body. His hands felt heavy as they came to rest on her shoulders.

'You love me...' In profile it was hard to read his expression, but she could feel the explosive tension coiled in his lean body.

Lily's eyes lifted.

'When I first saw you...'

Lily nodded encouragingly. 'In the restaurant that night,' she prompted.

'No, earlier in the day in Baeza.'

'Baeza!'

'You were sitting outside a café drinking wine.'

'You saw me there?'

He nodded. 'You were wearing this long floaty dress in white. Your hair was tied back here.' He touched the nape of her neck. 'You looked like a sad, sinfully sexy angel,' he recalled, pushing his fingers deep into the slippery thick-

ness of her shining hair and pressing a long, lingering kiss
to her soft pink lips. He stayed there with his nose brushing
the side of her, his breath warm on her cheek. Lily didn't
move; she didn't want this magical moment to end. Part of
her was a little afraid that she might wake up and discover
this had all been a dream.

His expression suggested that the memory was painful
for him. 'I was totally blown away, Lily.'

'You were…?' Lily wanted to believe him more than she
had ever wanted anything in her life. She was almost there,
but that last leap in the dark scared her. 'You know, you
don't have to say what you think I want to hear. I'll love
you anyway.'

'And I will spend the rest of my life trying to be worthy
of that love.'

A dry sob escaped her aching throat as she let her head
fall forward onto his shoulder. 'I can't believe this is happening.'

Santiago placed a finger under her chin and forced her
face up to his. Holding her eyes, he moved until his mouth
was positioned over hers and then slowly…very
slowly…he moved forward until their lips were sealed. Lily
gave a little shudder, moaned into his mouth and pressed
herself against him.

'Do you believe it's happening now?'

Lily let her fingers remain where they were tangled in
his hair. 'Something is happening,' she whispered. 'I'm just
not sure what.'

'I thought I was dreaming when I saw you,' he told her
huskily. 'I had never seen anything so beautiful in my life.'
He gave a shuddering sigh. 'I think I fell in love with you
at that moment.' He reached out and touched a finger to
the tear running down her cheek.

'But if I made such an impression why did you ignore me later that night in the restaurant?'

'Ignoring you was not my intention when I followed you back…'

A look of blank astonishment swept across her face. 'You followed me back in the taxi…?' Her nervous tension found release in a shaky laugh. 'You're not serious…?'

'I was very serious,' he promised her. 'You don't think I was about to lose the woman of my dreams, do you? Of course I followed you back, but between watching you walk into the hotel and seeing you in the bar I had learnt that you were newly widowed. My plan was to be sensitive, and take things slowly…respect your need to grieve…' His smile was loaded with self-mockery as he turned his head and met her amazed eyes.

'We both know that things didn't exactly go to plan. My self-control has never failed me in the past, but it was not robust enough to withstand the sight of you wet in that black swimsuit. I told myself that another man might see you in that swimsuit, a man not so sensitive, and then where would my patience get me? When love is involved it is possible to rationalise any decision.'

'You don't have to tell me that. Did you…was what your mother said true? Did you really ring her and say…?'

'That I had met the woman I was going to marry?' He nodded. 'Yes, I did.'

'That doesn't sound like something you would do.'

'It wasn't something I would do. You know, when I was young I used to swear that I would never marry. I never wanted to put a woman through what I saw my mother suffer.'

The pain in his eyes made her want to hug him. Her eyes widened as she realised with a sense of shock that she could. She touched the side of his face lightly with her hand

and when he looked down she kissed him on the mouth. It lacked the passion they had shared earlier, but the tenderness as his lips returned the pressure brought a lump to her throat.

When they drew a little apart she left her hand on his cheek. 'Your parents' marriage wasn't good?'

'He had a series of affairs, and he wasn't discreet. He seemed to take pleasure from rubbing my mother's nose in it. It was my fear that I had inherited a genetic propensity to hurt women. Then I learned I hadn't inherited anything at all from him—after the first shock it was actually quite a relief.' His self-recriminatory gaze lifted to hers. 'He made me loathe people who cheat on their partners, which is probably what made me go over the top when I found out you were married.' His eyes closed. 'God, when I think what a judgemental idiot I must have sounded...' His head dropped into his hands and he groaned.

Lily stroked his dark head. She couldn't bear the note of bitter self-recrimination in his voice. 'It wasn't your fault!' she exclaimed. 'I knew I shouldn't have, but when it comes to you I just can't be trusted.'

His head lifted. 'No...'

'It's true. I have no will-power around you and my sense of morality gets dangerously skewed.' Which might be handy, considering the role she was taking on. 'You know, I'm going to enjoy being your mistress.' She gave a little grimace. 'Sorry about blurting it out in front of your family that way. I'll be more discreet in future,' she promised earnestly.

'*Mistress!*' he echoed, looking at her as though she'd gone mad. 'What are you talking about? I don't want you to be my mistress. I never wanted you to be my mistress. I want you to be my wife.'

The look of frozen astonishment on her face slowly gave way to one of rapturous joy. 'You want to marry me?'

He framed her face with his hands. 'Of course I want to marry you.' He laughed. 'I love you, *querida*, I always will, and I can't imagine my life without you.'

'But don't you think that if I've cheated once I'd do it again?'

'No, never. I'd trust you with my life.'

The sentiment and the raw sincerity in his voice made Lily's eyes fill.

'Do you remember where we were before we were rudely interrupted?'

She sniffed and wiped the tears from her cheeks, responding to the wicked gleam in his eye with a smile of her own. 'Roughly,' she admitted.

'I was always told that a man should finish what he starts. It is character-building.'

With a sigh Lily looped her arms around his neck and dragged his dark head down to hers. 'What about a woman finishing?'

A broad grin slit his dark face. 'Oh, a gentleman always lets the lady finish first.' He watched the hot colour spread across her face as she got his meaning. 'Does that blush stop or does it go all over?'

Lily lifted her chin. 'There's one way you could find out.'

It was an invitation that Santiago was not about to refuse. With his bride-to-be in his arms, he took the stairs two at a time.

EPILOGUE

'COME on, Lily, the photographer's waiting.'

'Coming,' Lily shouted to Angel, who was already running out onto the terrace where the rest of the guests were gathered.

Lily's eyes were drawn towards the gilt-framed photo on the baby grand. She hoped the photographer would be as successful in capturing the spirit of the day as he had been a year ago when that had been taken.

She picked it up and looked at the glowing bride gazing up at her handsome husband. She must have been one of the few brides who had been congratulated on putting on ten pounds for her wedding day. The only person who hadn't been delighted had been the poor dress designer, who had been horrified at the final fitting when she hadn't been able to get the zip of the glorious silk gown up. Santiago, she recalled, had been particularly pleased she had regained her curvaceous figure.

It had been the happiest day of her life. So happy she hadn't believed Santiago when he had promised they had better days to look forward to.

He had been right and this was one of them, a very special one: the christening of their son, Raul.

'They're waiting for you, Lily.'

Lily lifted her head and smiled at Santiago, who stood there with their baby son in his arms.

She replaced the photo and tiptoed towards him. 'He looks like an angel,' she said, peeking at the dark-haired bundle.

'Yes,' agreed the proud father. 'But wait until they point a camera at him. He will start howling his lungs out,' he predicted. 'Just as he did during the service.' The church had echoed to ear-splitting shrieks.

'You're probably right.' She glanced back towards the photo. 'Does it seem like a year to you since we got married? Such a lot has happened. You know, I'm so happy it scares me sometimes,' she confided, lifting a hand lovingly to his face.

Santiago's eyes travelled from the child in his arms to the face of the woman he loved and he smiled. 'Don't be scared, *querida*. I will always be there for you.'

Lily, her heart full to bursting, blinked away a happy tear. He had been there for her during her pregnancy, soothing away her fears that fate would again rob them of the child they so desperately wanted. 'And I'll always be there for you, my love, and we'll both always be there for this little one,' she said, touching the dark head of their much-wanted baby. 'You know, I once thought I was unlucky. Now I know that I'm the luckiest woman alive!'

REQUEST YOUR FREE BOOKS!

HARLEQUIN® Presents®

2 FREE NOVELS PLUS 2 FREE GIFTS!

PASSION GUARANTEED SEDUCTION

YES! Please send me 2 FREE Harlequin Presents® novels and my 2 FREE gifts. After receiving them, if I don't wish to receive any more books, I can return the shipping statement marked "cancel." If I don't cancel, I will receive 6 brand-new novels every month and be billed just $3.80 per book in the U.S., or $4.47 per book in Canada, plus 25¢ shipping and handling per book and applicable taxes, if any*. That's a savings of close to 15% off the cover price! I understand that accepting the 2 free books and gifts places me under no obligation to buy anything. I can always return a shipment and cancel at any time. Even if I never buy another book from Harlequin, the two free books and gifts are mine to keep forever.

106 HDN EEXK 306 HDN EEXV

Name _____ (PLEASE PRINT) _____

Address _____ Apt. # _____

City _____ State/Prov. _____ Zip/Postal Code _____

Signature (if under 18, a parent or guardian must sign)

Mail to the Harlequin Reader Service®:

IN U.S.A.	**IN CANADA**
P.O. Box 1867	P.O. Box 609
Buffalo, NY	Fort Erie, Ontario
14240-1867	L2A 5X3

Not valid to current Harlequin Presents subscribers.

Want to try two free books from another line?
Call 1-800-873-8635 or visit www.morefreebooks.com.

* Terms and prices subject to change without notice. NY residents add applicable sales tax. Canadian residents will be charged applicable provincial taxes and GST. This offer is limited to one order per household. All orders subject to approval. Credit or debit balances in a customer's account(s) may be offset by any other outstanding balance owed by or to the customer. Please allow 4 to 6 weeks for delivery.

HARLEQUIN *Presents*

MISTRESS To A MILLIONAIRE

She's in his bedroom,
but he can't buy her love…

Showered with diamonds,
draped in exquisite lingerie,
whisked around the world…

**The ultimate fantasy becomes
a reality in Harlequin Presents,
with new author Annie West!**

If Marina poses as Ronan Carlisle's mistress,
he will ensure the man who has brought both
of them misery gets what he deserves. But why
would rich, eligible Ronan want Marina?

MISTRESS FOR THE TAKING
by Annie West

is available January 2007.

**More from this miniseries
coming in March!**

HARLEQUIN *Presents*

POSH DOCS

Dedicated, daring and devastatingly
handsome—these doctors are guaranteed
to raise your temperature!

The new collection by your favorite authors, available in January 2007:

HER BABY SECRET by Kim Lawrence
THE GREEK CHILDREN'S DOCTOR by Sarah Morgan
HER HONORABLE PLAYBOY by Kate Hardy
SHEIKH SURGEON by Meredith Webber